A
BUTTERFLY
NET AND A
KINGDOM

AND

OTHER STORIES

BOOKS BY BLAIR FULLER

A Far Place
Zebina's Mountain

ACKNOWLEDGMENTS

These stories appeared in the following publications:

"A Butterfly Net and a Kingdom" in a book called *Three Short Novels* (Random House); "Bakti's Hand" in *Massachusetts Review* and *O. Henry Prize Stories 1973*; "Alphonse" in *Way*; "Markle and the Mouse" in *The Paris Review*; "All Right" in *Silver Vain* and *O. Henry Prize Stories 1978*; "Education in Gotham" in *Nugget*; "A New Ocean" in *ZYZZYVA*; and "Some Rich Miles" in *California Living*.

A BUTTERFLY NET AND A KINGDOM

AND

OTHER STORIES
BLAIR FULLER

Creative Arts Book Company

Berkeley ■ 1989

Copyright ©1989 Blair Fuller

For information contact:

Creative Arts Book Company
833 Bancroft Way
Berkeley, California 94710

Typography: Renée King
Cover Design: Charles Fuhrman
Cover Illustration: Dugald Stermer
Text Design: Lynn Meinhardt

LIBRARY OF CONGRESS
Library of Congress Cataloging-in-Publication Data

Fuller, Blair.
    A butterfly net and a kingdom and other stories / Blair Fuller.
        p.   cm.
    ISBN 0-88739-065-X (pbk.) : $8.95
    I. Title
PS3556.U36B8 1988
813'.54—dc19   88-12082
                                                                CIP

Printed in the United States of America.

CONTENTS

A BUTTERFLY NET
AND A KINGDOM

S ellier had found the inevitable mistake in the preparation
of his current account with SCOA, the giant trading
company, and had looked up to curse the African clerk responsible when, through the propped-open shutters at the
front of the room, he saw Froelicher for the first time, butterfly net in hand, bareheaded, followed by two blacks carrying
a battered suitcase and a square black box on their heads.
Sellier, who wore his canvas porkpie hat indoors as well
as out every day until sundown, watched this greenhorn
or madman get directions from someone at the truck pool
and pass warehouses three and four before he decided to
go out on the verandah to meet him. If the man were truly
insane he did not want to talk with him in front of the
clerks.

Froelicher, short, wiry, middle-aged, with a shock of sandy
hair glinting in the sun, was looking from left to right at
the tin-roofed bungalows and workshops which lined the

puddled street. Then he saw Sellier and waved. Sellier remained motionless, hands on hips, a spittle-darkened Gauloise drooping from the corner of his mouth. Froelicher jumped the two steps to the verandah and said, "My name's Froelicher. I'm happy to meet you," in mildly accented French.

"Sellier," shaking hands.

"Oh, I knew that." Froelicher's tanned face burst into a smile, his face crinkling into dozens of lines. It seemed years since Sellier had been given such a smile. "I knew that, Mr. Sellier. The man who made a garden of the forest? The man who made Galoa rich? Why, they talk about you from here to Monrovia. I knew you the moment I saw you."

Sellier grunted. "German?"

"German name, but I'm Danish."

"You've come from Monrovia?"

"That's right."

Sellier's trucks had suspended hauling for the rainy season and almost no one else used the road. "Who brought you?"

"I walked."

"Walked? One hundred and thirty miles? In the rainy season?"

"Yes. Took me three weeks and a pair of shoes." He pointed to his sandals whose soles were cut from used automobile tires and laughed a high, but hearty, laugh.

Sellier said, "I see," and his lips drew back into a shrewd, almost affectionate, little sneer, well known to his subordinates, which said *now* I understand you.

What he understood was that Froelicher was a fugitive. Over the years quite a number of them had turned up in Galoa—men who had fled to Liberia from the penalties or the records of their crimes in Europe only to commit some new offense there and be forced to flee again. Galoa, Sellier's fief, was perhaps the one spot in the world where liberty was available to them; the place was so entirely Sellier's creation and its control was so firmly in his hands that if he saw usefulness in the man, papers were unmentioned and the man stayed on. Five now worked as clerks and mechanics for him. They worked hard and he paid them suitably. They worked hard or he wrote the French police in Kankan who came down and arrested the laggard and ignored the others. Sellier had had to write only two such letters.

He supposed he should have recognized Froelicher immediately for what he was, but the man's frank, even gay, demeanor had confused him. An insane fugitive this time, perhaps. "Are you looking for work?" Sellier asked.

"Oh, no, Mr. Sellier," Froelicher laughed. "Just a courtesy call. I have my work."

"And what's that?"

"I'm a Fellow of the Royal Dutch and British Museums, a naturalist, a collector of specimens."

"What brings you to Galoa?"

"Luck," said Froelicher, beaming. "And what luck! This," he waved a hand in the air, "this is *paradise.*"

Sellier was so astounded that he did not even grunt. Later, he told the anecdote many times in the bars and restaurants of Kankan and Conakry, always to incredulous hilarity at the word "paradise," but at the time he was shocked speechless. Finally he managed, "You think so?"

"Oh, yes! I've never seen such a profusion of life! You've got scorpions around here as big as that—maybe six, seven inches long—biggest I ever saw. A tremendous variety of snakes and monkeys. And your butterflies!"

"My butterflies?"

"Well, they're yours if you want them."

Froelicher's smile restored Sellier's aplomb. "Won't you come inside?"

"Just got to pay off these boys." Which he did with very little money, handshakes, and laughter all around. "Nice boys," he said as they walked away. "They came quite a stretch with me ohing and ahing at the things I caught as though they'd never seen them before." He picked up his suitcase and when Sellier reached for the black box said, "Easy does it, please. That's my microscope, Mr. Sellier."

The clerks all stared at the butterfly net as Sellier led Froelicher to his desk and pulled up the visitor's chair. Like the rest of the furniture in town, it had been made to Sellier's specifications in the shop. It was of solid mahogany, straight-backed and armless, and its seat was three inches lower than that of Sellier's chair. Froelicher sat down and Sellier picked up the SCOA account, took it to the delinquent clerk, and punched the

incorrect figures with his forefinger. "Idiot, son of a goat...
impossible to teach you anything. Copy it over." He slapped the
clerk on the ear. Sitting down behind his desk he shoved his hat
to the back of his head, worked the Gauloise from his lip and
lit a fresh one, then smiling faintly said to Froelicher, "I'll never
get used to it. Never."

Froelicher nodded. After a pause he said, "You're way up there,
aren't you? The seat, I mean. You're sitting way up there, like on
a throne."

No one had ever dared comment on Sellier's little advantage.
"How long do you wish to stay in Galoa?"

"Maybe the rest of my life."

They agreed that Froelicher should be Sellier's guest for the
first few days. One of the clerks took him to the bungalow, which
was empty except for the servants because, as Sellier said rather
proudly, "My wife's health can't stand the rainy season. I send
her home to Paris every year."

During their second breakfast together Froelicher broached
the subject of more permanent housing. "This is very kind of
you, Mr. Sellier. Don't think I'm not appreciative, but—"

"I'm looking around for you," Sellier interrupted. "Please be
patient."

By the end of the week he had checked Froelicher's story with
all the usual sources. He was not wanted by the Liberian police.
His passport had been in order at the Guinean frontier. Yes, a
white man had trekked through all the villages from here to
Monrovia, a man with a black juju bag and a net to catch flies,
a very funny man the natives had found him.

"There's some space in the European compound," Sellier said
that evening. "Just a room like the others for the single men. You
can have it if you like."

"How much is the rent?"

"It's yours for nothing."

"I don't know if I can accept that, Mr. Sellier. That's too
generous." But the next evening, after he had inspected the place,
he refused it for different reasons. "I'm afraid it's too small, not
enough room for my specimens and things. Now I've been
walking around the countryside every day—marvelous, in-
cidentally, what you've accomplished here—and I found a hut

just up the road a little. You've surely seen it many times. Roof kind of falling down? On a little knoll? No one's lived in it for some time, and I wonder if I might move in there?"

"I know the place."

"I went through it this afternoon, actually, and I think I could fix up that roof in a couple of days. The walls are all right and there's a good fresh stream nearby."

"You want to live like a native," Sellier said sadly.

Froelicher shrugged and beamed. "That's what I did coming up here."

Sellier did not want him to. It lessened the natives' respect to see a white man gone bush. But lying in bed that night he could think of no way to prevent his doing so. None of the levers he held against the other Europeans of the town—money, advancement, accommodations, leave—were of any use against Froelicher. And there wasn't an empty bungalow in town with which to buy him off. Perhaps he could have got rid of him by explaining what sort of dignity he thought Europeans should maintain and relying on Froelicher's gratitude for the hospitality already shown him, but he felt uncertain of Froelicher's reactions and, furthermore, he realized with surprise, he liked the man and wanted him to stay. He was refreshing and original in an all too familiar scene. Perhaps he was truly original; Sellier could no longer judge. And although a few years ago Froelicher's plant would have seriously worried him, now he was only fretful. The business had grown until it had its own momentum. For the Africans it had created new habits, new conveniences, new possibilities, which they wouldn't lightly put aside. If Froelicher's presence was disruptive, the disruption would be gradual. Sellier would have the time to find a pretext.

Four nights later when the hut's roof had been repaired the two men had a parting dinner. Sellier had two bottles of Pouilly Fuisse in the refrigerator and yesterday's plane had brought fresh sole from the coast of Britanny and endives for the salad.

Froelicher seemed overjoyed by the meal. "If I ate and drank like this every night, Mr. Sellier, I'd never catch another specimen. Be dead in no time! Just wonderful."

There were crepes for dessert. They drank their coffee in silence until Froelicher asked, "What was it like when you first saw it, Mr. Sellier? Galoa, I mean, fifteen years ago?"

Sellier grunted. "A road down from Kankan that was hardly passable, even in the dry season. At the end of it an African reseller with a drum of kerosene and a little gunpowder. They made their own rifles then. Once in a while you still see one, cap and ball. He had a little grease for the hair, a few ribbons. Not much of anything came out of here."

"Isn't that marvelous! What you've done!"

"You've said that before, but why should a naturalist think these changes such a marvel?"

"Oh," said Froelicher, "if the government makes a few preserves and parks in the next few years the forest will last forever— should anyways, just as it is. The forest doesn't need me, but the people here need you."

"Four hundred tons of coffee last year and seven hundred of cocoa. Next year maybe a fifth again as much. That's money." Sellier knew that these tonnages had not materialized as a reaction to the people's needs, but the interpretation, which had never occurred to him, was pleasing.

"Sure," said Froelicher. "Money and roads and a post office and even airplanes, for heaven's sake. How did you start?"

Sellier considered the ceiling. He rarely thought of the past or had to tell its story since everyone in the colony knew it. Instead he criticized the present or visualized the future. Now he collected his memories. "We bought an old truck from SCOA—that's my partner, Gaux and I. It was a Panhard made in nineteen twenty-seven. He and I worked for SCOA, you see, and when business went flat in nineteen forty they wanted to ship us back to France. We resigned. We were kids, twenty-four and twenty-five, but we'd done two tours out here and we had ambition. He was assistant cocoa buyer for the house. I was in merchandise. When we arrived here we lived as you're going to— in a hut. It drove me crazy, to be frank. Then we got our first store built and moved in there. Not luxury but a great improvement. We ran that old truck all through the war, up to the railhead at Kankan with what produce we could find and back with merchandise. We ran it on benzine, anything we could get.

Eventually, we converted it to wood. We knew how to work. And whatever we made we put back in—into coffee and cocoa. We got the natives to make plantations. By the end of the war we had something to sell." He had omitted from the story that at the time of their resignations from SCOA he and Gaux had expected to be called up by the army. As it turned out they had not had to dodge a call but they had been prepared to do so.

"What became of the African, the reseller?"

"Who? Oh, Father Mamadou. He sells gas and kerosene for me. He's done well. Has a plantation, too."

"And Gaux?"

"I bought him out five years ago." Sellier did not like to remember it. "Brandy?"

"With pleasure." After a sip Froelicher said, "I've got a confession to make, Mr. Sellier. Don't worry, it's nothing serious. You probably won't like it but it isn't going to do you any harm. Won't do you any good either—that's for me, the good. Thing's been on my conscience and I'd like to clear it up before I leave your house." He got up, went through the door to his room, and returned carrying a tin box. "Now the first thing is that this is your box. A box for crackers. I just dumped them out, don't know what happened to them. Maybe the boys ate them. Anyway, I stole your crackers. Now, stay where you are and just sit still." He laid the box on its side on the floor and pried off the lid. Out slid a large scorpion. Sellier recoiled but remained sitting. "And the second thing is this beautiful creature here. She's one of the finest specimens I've seen. Actually I don't know her sex, I just think of scorpions as she's." Froelicher had straightened up and was staring at Sellier who watched the scorpion move in small, regular circles, occasionally stopping and raising its vicious tail. "She isn't all I've got, Mr. Sellier, but judging by your face I'd better not show you the rest. I've got several other specimens—well, I won't go into it. Anyway—"

"Your foot!"

Froelicher moved his leg slightly without looking down. "Anyway, I want to apologize. I knew you wouldn't want these things in your house and I brought them in just the same. Couldn't resist them. They'll all be gone in the morning. There now, I've said it. I'll just pick her up and take her off to bed."

He knelt and coaxed the scorpion back into the tin with a table knife.

When the lid was safely on, Sellier uttered a series of grunts which only after a time Froelicher understood to be laughter. "I'm glad you can laugh about it, Mr. Sellier. Frankly, I wasn't sure you would."

Sellier shook his head, still laughing.

"Good night, Mr. Sellier. I feel badly about this and I'm going to ask whoever it is up there, or down there, or wherever, to forgive me. I'll do that, anyway." He disappeared into his room and closed the door.

When Sellier had managed to stop his laughter he turned off the dining-room lights and went to his study. The desk lamp cast a yellow shimmer on the nylon screening which separated the study from the rest of the verandah and glinted on the copper screens that enclosed the bungalow. He looked at the moldings and at the corners of the ceiling. Not a mosquito, not a lizard or a roach—it was as clean as a ceiling in France. I thought of the detailed planning and work that had gone into the bungalow's construction—the concrete underflooring, the aluminum frame windows, the lawn hand-planted tuft by tuft—all to keep out Africa, to live unbothered by the myriad flying things and the stupid snakes and lizards and scorpions which worked themselves into unlikely places. All that thought and expense and ranting at the builders only to have this mad Dane smuggle that world in with him in little boxes! He laughed again, and remembered the hut he and Gaux had first occupied—the insects rustling in the thatch all night long and the spiders with bodies as big as his thumb dangling over his nose at dawn, the careful examination he had given the floor every morning before getting up from his cot.

Gaux had hung a sign by the doorway of that hut: TIME IS MONEY. If it hadn't been they wouldn't have remained an extra minute.

Any spot of earth had been a toilet and at every toilet the flies swarmed, flies so vicious they left round bleeding indentations in the skin. He had never got used to it. How could anyone? And later, in their first bungalow, he remembered the dozens of lazy pink lizards on the walls, waiting for the bugs to fly into their mouths; with that little effort they had gorged themselves. The swifter, yellow and brown ones who ran around the floor needed to extend themselves only a little more to catch the roaches. Screens had been unknown at the time. As the business had grown he and Gaux had built new quarters, always for themselves, passing on the old ones to the Europeans who came on contract to work for them. Each house had in some way improved on the last. He had noted a few minor inconveniences in this one for the day when he would have to build another.

Sellier would have Froelicher's room fumigated in the morning after he had gone. If he hadn't left Galoa after a couple of weeks in his hut, Sellier would be much surprised.

But every other day or so when Sellier saw him in the street or at the provisions store, Froelicher was smiling or laughing, and the other Europeans and even the Africans were smiling too—probably with surprise at the sight of so cheerful a white man.

"How goes it, Froelicher?"

"Very *well*, Mr. Sellier. *Very* well. Getting the place fixed. Pretty comfortable now. I can't tell you how grateful I am to you for letting me use it. Just suits me fine. I hope you'll come over and see it."

"I will." But for several weeks something always prevented Sellier's doing so. When finally he went, Froelicher had indeed succeeded in transforming the place. The path from the road was cleared and the area around the cooking fire was packed and swept clean. Most of the thatch was yellow-new and the mud walls had been freshly whitewashed. Sellier called and Froelicher poked his head out, sweeping aside the burlap sack that served as a door.

"Well, Mr. Sellier, I certainly am glad to see you. It seemed as though the place wasn't baptized or something until you paid a visit." He rubbed one eye with the heel of a hand, shaking Sellier's with the other. "Excuse me. I was just taking a nap. Been out in the woods since dawn. Come in."

Standing still, while his eyes grew accustomed to the dimness, Sellier felt the chill dampness rising along his shins and the heat of his breath dispelling the cool around his face. He had forgotten that thatch made such good insulation. His eyes first picked out a hammock of vines and reeds slung in the corner of his right, then, along the wall in front of him an impoverished working space, crates and boxes neatly fitted together to form a platform for the microscope and a bookcase and shelves for a variety of bottles and tins. Several boards of mounted butterflies stood against the wall nearby.

"I plan to get a few more things. I'll find a comfortable chair somewhere to offer you next time."

"Very tidy."

"Couldn't help but be, could it? Froelicher laughed and led the way out of the hut. As he was pointing to a breadfruit tree at the far side of the clearing an African girl appeared, walking up the path from the stream with a pile of wet clothes in her arms. She was young, in her teens Sellier judged. Her skin was dark but her features were almost Caucasian. Perhaps she had Hausa blood. Froelicher said, "Here's Jenny, I couldn't make head or tail of her name, so I call her that. Isn't that right, Jenny?"

She dropped her eyes coquettishly and smiled.

As they watched her spreading out the clothes to dry on the tops of bushes Froelicher added, "Understands the name I've given her and not much else. Very pleasant, you know? Very relaxing."

"Where did she come from?"

"One of those little villages out that way," he waved an arm to the west. "I was around there exploring, seeing what there was, and she started following me. She has wonderful eyes, sees much better in the forest than I do, so I was glad to have her along. Another day I went out near there and the same thing happened, but that time she helped me bring back some specimens. Then she began turning up here and a couple of days ago she brought a little bundle of things with her, so I think she's going to stay."

Stiff-legged, Jenny bent to the ground for each piece of clothing. When she stood, her jumper hung straight from the points of her breasts. "She looks clean," Sellier said.

"I never saw anything like it, Mr. Sellier. Down there at the brook washing herself all the time. Once in a while she gives me a good scrubbing, too." She turned and smiled at his laughter.

"Well, Mr. Sellier, the doctors will tell you that celibacy won't do you any harm, but I never believed them. Once a week minimum is my motto."

The odd thing was, Sellier reflected, that although Froelicher was poor and far from handsome, it did not occur to him either that the man was bragging or that he had ever had difficulty fulfilling his motto's dictum. "I've got to be going," Sellier said. "Anything I can do for you?"

"Are you going to meet the plane tomorrow? If you are, I'd like to ride out with you. Got some specimens to put on the plane."

Sellier nodded. "Meet me at the office."

"Oh, and another thing. Are there any trucks running to Monrovia or Kankan? I'd like to ask one of the drivers to do something for me."

"Not for another three weeks. What do you need?"

"It's just a silly thing. I wanted to get Jenny a pair of high-heeled shoes. For a long time I couldn't figure out what her trouble was, kept sitting down and pointing at her heels and then standing up on her toes. She'll probably fall down and break her skull when she gets them, but that's what she wants." Again Jenny smiled when he laughed.

That night, on his way to bed after a lonely session in his study, Sellier opened the door to his wife's closet and looked over the row of highly polished shoes. All of them were of a certain kind—a kind that she would not wear in Paris—and most showed age despite their care. He picked up a pair of medium-high heels. Machine made and cheap; she had bought them in Conakry, no doubt, for in Paris her shoes were made to measure. He took them to his bed and sat wondering where she was and how she looked at this moment. In bed with her Jules? It was eleven-fifteen, perhaps not yet the hour in Paris. No she was probably in some *boite* absorbing the *chansonnier's* witticisms, dressed and made up in a manner he was never permitted fully to see. On her returns to Galoa, he caught glimpses of it—stockings of a fresh shade, eye shadow, and coiffes that showed a hairdresser's hand—but it soon disappeared. She quickly reassumed her African uniform of blouses with wide arm holes, cotton skirts, and walking shoes. After a few days, her hair was tied in back and her face shone.

When he joined her in Paris he got a more exact impression of worldly-Annette although he knew that his presence to some degree subdued her makeup and that there were dresses in her closet she would not wear during his stay, dresses which presented her breasts like fruits so perfectly ripe that they each deserved a decor. He grunted, remembering the inevitable sequence of conversations. On arrival he would ask her what she had been doing. She had been seeing a lot of the So-and-Sos. Within a day or two there would be a rendezvous with these So-and-Sos, usually couples on leave from Conakry or retired colonials, and at some point Mrs. So-and-So would say to him, "Annette was so lonely we took her everywhere with us." This ceremonial lie having been stated, Annette could describe amusements, restaurants, weekends in Normandy with equanimity—she had always been with the So-and-Sos.

Here in Galoa there was a different but just as inevitable progression. After a few months' residence she would remark that she had gained inches and pounds. "Just look!" and she would pinch a roll in her stomach to show him. Then she would diet and when she had regained what she considered her best shape she would feel ill, fatigued by the climate, and suggest it was advisable that she return to France. Sellier sometimes wondered whether she were getting in trim for the Jules she had left or in anticipation of a new conquest. On balance he inclined to the latter interpretation. Several times in Paris he believed he had spotted the current lover, each time a different man, through a glance exchanged or Annette's sudden vivacity. If he had divined correctly they were getting ever younger and would one day be the same age as Jacques—perhaps friends of Jacques', that would be pretty. Jacques was how old, now? Eleven? Sellier saw so little of him—a month or two a year following the spring rains—that he tended to forget. A fine boy, nevertheless, rugged like himself. Sellier would not let him dissipate that strength here in the tropics.

He turned the shoes in his hands, remembering the polished calluses on Annette's feet, the blue veins in the instep—the slender feet of which she was proud. He was lucky, as he had told himself many times, that literally within minutes of his first awareness of her infidelity he had realized that he had expected it to happen and did not care very much that it had. Both he and Gaux had married shortly after the war's end had made travel possible; Gaux to a barmaid he had found in Conakry, who hadn't lasted long, and he to Annette a few weeks after meeting her in Bordeaux. In retrospect the propriety of their courtship, the calls, the chaperones, amused him. His mother and father had nodded approval after the two families had been introduced and doubtless hers had nodded in identical fashion. They had married with a thin pretense of love and with a solid marriage contract filed; she in reality because he and Gaux were prospering and he because she had looked like civilization itself and would provide him with an heir. That, she had quickly done. He recognized that she had seized on his own attitude toward Africa as justification for her long stays in France—that in trying to protect her from the tropics he had opened the way for her Jules. But so be it. Now her presence irritated him as much as her absence.

She would not miss these shoes any more than she missed Galoa, or himself. He got up, found a box, and put them inside it.

At two o'clock the next afternoon Froelicher was sitting patiently on the verandah of Sellier's office with two cases marked *Animal Vivant Fragile* at his feet. From his desk Sellier could hear him amiably explaining their contents to whoever passed. "Yes, very deadly. Kills you in about thirty seconds. A beauty, this one."

If Sellier was distracted, the clerks were certain to be. He closed his desk and collected Froelicher and the cases. Getting into the jeep he felt under the seat for the shoe box, found it, hesitated, and then decided to wait until he dropped Froelicher at his path.

Little more than a year ago, over the strong opposition of larger towns, Sellier had got the administration to cut the airstrip. The Air France Conakry-Freetown-Monrovia flight came in once a week. Groups of Africans dotted each side of the runway and more were arriving, suddenly appearing out of apparently impenetrable forest. Some had trekked since dawn to see the "heaven-boat" come in, and many had brought their drums to celebrate its safe landing. As Sellier and Froelicher waited in the heat the Liberian Consul pedaled up beside them on his bicycle and said, "Good afternoon, sirs." When wearing his uniform which consisted of a three-cornered hat, a blue tailcoat with red piping, and a tinny-looking sword, he spoke nothing but English. The rest of the time, as a clerk in the provisions store, he spoke French like everyone else.

Froelicher said, "Good afternoon, Admiral."

"Liberian Consul, sir."

"Very sorry," said Froelicher. "A splendid uniform you have."

"We think to show dignity of Liberian nation."

"It certainly does," said Froelicher. "I'd say it did just that."

The consul was bare chested under his tailcoat and wore a pair of ragged shorts made from flour sacks. Sellier turned away to hide his amusement while Froelicher continued with apparent seriousness to question the consul about the historic origin of the costume, the circumstances of his appointment, and his duties. By the time the plane's motors were heard humming in the distance it was clear that Froelicher had won a friend.

Red dust plumed up as the Dakota's wheels touched down, and drumming from every quarter of the field mingled with the popping of the plane's exhaust. Women in a group near the jeep began to dance in a shuffling, chanting line and their children jigged around them. Froelicher walked over to them and suddenly, to Sellier's horror, added a sailor's hornpipe to the celebration. Sellier silently cursed the consul's grin and fixedly watched the plane as it taxied toward him. When it had cut its motors he permitted himself one glance. Froelicher was obscured by a circle of dancers.

As Sellier was getting the mail at the foot of the ramp Froelicher appeared at his side, panting, dripping sweat, and carrying his two cases. "Lord," he said, "I don't know why every one of them doesn't die of apoplexy. Do you, Mr. Sellier?"

Sellier did not answer.

But when he stopped the jeep by the path to Froelicher's hut he found he could not deliver the lecture on the necessity for white dignity that he had been preparing in his mind. Froelicher's pale eyes were clearly innocent although troubled by his companion's silence as he stood at the roadside and said thank you. Sellier pictured the hut and its meager collection of possessions, the girl and the nameless stews she must give him to eat. How little he has, Sellier thought, what few pleasures.

And instead of lecturing he reached under the seat for the box. "I have something for you," he said. "I found an old pair of my wife's shoes that might do for the girl."

"That's marvelous!" said Froelicher. "They'll do just fine. Come on up and we'll give them to her." Sellier obediently followed him up the path.

Jenny was squatting in the shade of a tree, chewing a stick of lemon wood and watching a pot steam over a small fire in the center of the clearing. She made a pleased "ah" sound and came smiling to meet them.

Froelicher said, "Jenny," then rapped on the box, pointed at Sellier, and handed it to her. As she took it her mouth hung open in a perfect O and it remained so while she turned the box around, examining all its sides. Finally, Froelicher lifted one end of the lid and she removed it. Her face showed such wonder and then such joy that Sellier felt he had never before seen such expressions, entirely pure in emotion and free from constraint. Then she remembered to thank him and the flash of immortality was gone, for she had to think of how to do it properly. Her body twisted with indecision; then she bowed to Sellier, murmuring, and glanced at Froelicher to see if she'd done rightly.

"I guess she won't put them on now," Froelicher said. "She'll just look at them a while." And Sellier saw in his smile, too, a touch—not so absolute as in hers, perhaps no European could attain that simplicity—just a touch of the same purity.

Sellier grunted and said good-bye.

"Thanks again."

On his way to the office Sellier wondered if he had ever seen an expression on Annette's face that was not to some extent willed, or heard her voice stripped of all conscious tones.

During Annette's and Jacques' visit of two and a half months following the rainy season Sellier was constantly irritated by her. All her usual complaints about the heat, the insects, the dullness of the other Europeans, the stupidity of Africans, annoyed him. Those features of their life had improved over the years, and while he still complained of them if they were strikingly bad, she seemed to do so by habit. "This awful humidity," she would say. "These idiots," when the humidity was not unusual and the servants were only a trifle slow. It was as though she had a checklist of expected grievances against which she must daily raise her voice.

Most annoying was her attitude toward Froelicher. Away from Galoa, to be sure, Sellier described him as an eccentric, an object of amusement, but Annette bluntly called him unhinged and thought him a menace to the community and particularly to Jacques who, as any boy would be, was fascinated by Froelicher's collection and by his methods of adding to it. She seemed deaf and blind to Froelicher's gaiety and originality and insisted that his way of life would corrupt their son. They exchanged many angry words about it; she wanted Sellier to forbid any contact between them. Sellier argued that the boy's interest was natural, that the scientific information he picked up would stand him in good stead, and that he was not going to forget his upbringing and become a good-for-nothing in a few short months. She remained so vehement that Sellier wondered briefly if she were not trying to throw him off the scent of an affair she and Froelicher were having. He was greatly relieved when she had lost her pounds and declared herself debilitated by the climate.

He was sorry to say good-bye to Jacques. Partly because of the boy's enthusiasm for nature Sellier had felt a stronger intimacy with him than ever before. But he would soon have had to return to school in any case.

After their visit, Sellier spoke differently of Froelicher, perhaps in reaction to what had seemed to him the injustice of Annette's view. Instead of an amusing, mad eccentric he pictured him as an eccentric but quite wonderful man who somehow managed to live happily in circumstances which would ruin the health and spirit of almost anyone else. Sellier even became a little proprietary about him, as though he had provided his quarters foreseeing that he would enrich the town's life.

Indeed, as the months passed, the attitudes of all the Europeans changed. Froelicher remained the town's amusement, but in some ways he became its wise man as well. For one thing, he was a useful intermediary between black and white. He never interceded in matters of business—debts owed, positions or advancements wanted—which the Africans often asked him to do, but he did smooth over many personal frictions which otherwise might have been bitter. For example, early in November a village girl gave birth to a son whose father was one of the fugitives in permanent residence. The pair had not lived together, she had merely visited his room twice a week until too pregnant to do so, and when her visits had stopped he had found a replacement and ignored her condition. Her tribal brothers were angry, and since most of them worked for Sellier the situation was potentially unsettling. Two of them explained the matter to Froelicher, and one noon he was waiting for the father at the gate to the truck pool where he worked as a master mechanic.

"Hello there, Crespin."

"Hello, Froelicher." He was a tall, small-boned man who would have been slight if manual labor had not added bunches of muscles to his shoulders, arms, and chest. His eyes, set close together, were at once wary and condescending.

"Got something I'd like to talk to you about," Froelicher said. "Will you walk along with me?"

Crespin did not answer but started walking.

"Now I don't want to butt into your business," Froelicher hesitated, ducking his head as though swallowing something bulky, "but that's just what I'm going to do. I don't know if you know it, but you're the father of a son."

"How do you know it's mine? I don't."

"She says it is; anyway it doesn't make any difference. Don't get the wrong impression. There's nothing bad about this, this is wonderful!" And Froelicher laughed.

"Wonderful?"

"Sure. She's pleased. Her family's pleased. The whole village is pleased as punch. They think red babies are lucky—he looks brown to me but they call them red. They think he'll grow up as smart as Sellier and get twice as rich. You don't have to worry about that baby. He'll be taken care of fine."

"Then what is it?"

"Well, now this is the point. I believe you were a forger?"

Crespin flushed and spat. Everyone knew each other's stories but by unspoken agreement they were never mentioned to their subjects.

"Never mind," said Froelicher. "It doesn't make any difference. But, supposing you were a forger, I should imagine you would have been gratified by professional appreciation of your work.

It must be a satisfaction to get the bad check, or whatever, passed, but to hear a fellow forger say you'd done a beautiful job on that check—I imagine that would be the deepest satisfaction. You'd know by his saying so that you'd really learned your art. Isn't that right?"

"Perhaps."

"Well, in this case what's wanted of you is the same sort of thing. The people of the village and the girl would like you to go out there, look at the boy, and say, 'Fine baby! Looks just like my grandfather who owned half of France.' You know? Just pat it on the head—not on top, kind of soft on top—but on the side, and say he's perfect. Because it's the father's word that counts with them. If the father doesn't say anything they think something's wrong."

"That's all?" Crespin stopped walking and peered at Froelicher. "That's all I have to do?"

"Just that. Easiest thing in the world. I could go out there with you since you probably don't know where it is."

Crespin started walking again in silence. There was no clear reason not to do as Froelicher suggested, but he did not know where such an acknowledgment might lead him. Finally he said, "I take my orders from Sellier. You can talk to him about it and if he says for me to go, I'll go."

"I don't want to bother Sellier with this. Good Lord, he's a busy man. Don't want to mix him up in a little thing like this."

"Talk to Sellier."

Froelicher followed him, arguing, until Crespin's door was shut between them.

Night after night Froelicher waited for him at quitting time and reopened the discussion. The spectacle was absurd, wiry little Froelicher skipping along beside the larger man, waving his arms and expostulating and repeatedly having the door shut in his face. But by the end of the week the absurdity, which was naturally Froelicher's, had in large part become his adversary's. Crespin listened to jokes about his qualities as a stud and about the intervention of the "godfather" all day long in the shop. The remarks angered him and once he took a punch at Froelicher, but the blow missed and he was roughed up by two of his colleagues. Worn out by the teasing and the setting of the tide against him, Crespin finally gave in.

The visit was easily passed after all, and on his return Crespin found to his surprise that the new jokes at his expense were soon forgotten and that in some measure the incident had made him an expert on tribal life. He was asked many questions about the attitude of the girl and the reception that her parents and the village had given him. He even took friends out to see the boy on occasional Sundays. The outcome of the episode pleased everyone.

Another thing that changed Froelicher's position in the town was his assumption of the role of medical man. The nearest doctor was some hundred miles away in Kankan, and for many years Sellier had kept the first-aid box and dispensed the quinine and the antifungicide. He had always resented the amount of time these small services consumed and was content to pass them on, together with a small salary which Froelicher was happy to have. Due to his extensive knowledge of physiology he could perform small operations. He lanced boils, sewed cuts, and cured ingrown toenails. White and black flocked to him for their ailments and the bills for medical supplies quickly doubled, but Sellier did not complain. Froelicher was under orders to treat none but emergency cases during business hours, and better health should produce better work.

Now that Froelicher was on the payroll the other Europeans felt a new familiarity with him. Some of them because they had been struck by the disparity between the two men's personalities and others out of mischief or a vague wish for an ally spoke bitterly to Froelicher of their boss: "He's got a bankbook for a heart," "He'd work his grandmother to death if he had her signature on a contract," and so on.

Froelicher deflected these remarks. "You've had your experience with Mr. Sellier, and I've had mine. You have your opinion; I have mine. All I can say is that no man has been so generous to me as Sellier has. As far as I'm concerned he couldn't be a better or a kinder man."

One day, to a particularly tedious list of grievances, Froelicher replied, "He supports you, doesn't he? He supports everyone here, isn't that right? It seems to me everyone here is very much in his debt. Look what he's done: he's created wealth where there wasn't any, jobs where there weren't any; he's opened up a whole little part of the world to commerce; he's built a school; he's shown the Africans how to work in a disciplined way. You tell me he promised to have a refrigerator for you two months ago and it hasn't turned up yet. I say on balance that's nothing."

Even those who most resented his making their gripes seem petty could not stay angry long. In a week or so they would be back at the hut grateful for Froelicher's attentions, interested by the new specimen he was always delighted to show, and amused by the two white-bearded monkeys he kept as pets and by the spectacle of Jenny tipping around the rough clearing on her high heels.

Annette stayed in Paris more than three months, returning after the New Year when the "little" rains of December had passed.

Now that the roads were passable the trading season opened. The bright red, perfectly conditioned two-and-a-half-ton Fords were continually on the road between Galoa and Monrovia, taking down the coffee and cocoa and bringing back most of the supplies needed for the entire year. The operation demanded constant surveillance and there were frequent mishaps—under- and overloadings, failures of ordered goods to arrive in Monrovia, pilferage, and truck breakdowns on the rough dirt highway. Daily telegrams from Paris informed Sellier of cocoa and coffee prices. Cocoa had been falling for several years and Sellier did not foresee an upturn. He shipped three quarters of the crop as quickly as he could, selling it on arrival, freight-alongside, Monrovia.

The coffee was a different matter. During the last six months its price had fluctuated widely and as the season opened it rose slightly, fell, and rose again. Sellier held back. He began to ship the crop but stored it at dockside, deciding he would pay storage until he got his price. Toward the end of the season the price climbed. It leveled off short of the figure Sellier had hoped for, then started falling. He sold and within two weeks the price had jumped above what he had wanted. He cursed himself for behaving like a frightened greenhorn.

"I'm sure many others did worse," Annette said, trying to cheer him in so perfunctory a manner that he felt angered.

"There are always idiots."

"You'll admit it's a profitable year, all the same."

"If I'd held on just two more weeks there'd be an extra dollar for every soul in Galoa."

"Oh, you're an altruist now?"

She understood perfectly well that he had not meant he would distribute the extra profits; the word "altruist" incensed him. "I always have been for you and Jacques. Sometimes for your family."

"Charming! You bring that up again!"

It was a bad fight, one of their worst. Two days later she said, "I'm going back to Paris. My health, you know." Her tone was sarcastic and he was suddenly aware that this time she had neither gained nor lost her weight. Their break was in the open.

The rains fell on schedule. Sellier sat alone in his screened office every evening hearing its intermittent roar. He was not so pressed by work now and often raised his eyes from the ledgers and the maps simply to feel the air and sense the town around him. He thought often of Gaux, at first of the bitterness of their parting and then of the good years of their partnership. For a long time he had managed not to remember Gaux's ravaged, doleful face at their last meeting or to compare his present situation with their early years together. But now he found that the memories did not sting. Gaux had been worn out, had given in, until he had not only lost all forward momentum but had permitted every kind of sloppiness in the routine work and in his personal life. Obese, drunk at midday—even Gaux must understand by now that for the good of the business and the community Sellier had had to force him out. And no matter what anyone thought or said, he had paid Gaux a fair price for ten of his fifty-percent interest and remitted regularly on the forty percent he had allowed him to keep. There was nothing on Sellier's conscience, but a sorrow invaded his soul. Like the captain of a ship he kept a certain distance from his subordinates, even from Daygrand, his second in command. Only Gaux had been his equal, and during the good years they had shared everything. Now, perhaps because he could no longer pretend that his marriage contained any intimacy, not even the intimacy of understood duplicity, his companionship with Gaux seemed nearly a need.

Peripheral as he was to it, Froelicher was the one person in town with whom equality could be afforded. Sellier visited him more often, leaving the office before sundown, a rare event in the past, and spending an hour or so of daylight playing chess with him and discussing the collection.

"*B. Nasicornis*, the nose-horned viper. Call them horned vipers usually, but the real ones are up north in the desert. Best one I've had." Froelicher coaxed the sluggish, red and yellow, diamond-backed snake out of its box with a short stick, then laughed. "A couple of months ago I had one; sent it home to my father as a present. I wrote him I'd pulled its fangs out, you know, and what does he do but let it loose in the living room! Hah! Left it loose there for a couple of weeks, children, all kinds of people walking in and out. Any damned fool ought to know the fangs grow back in six days!" Froelicher slapped his thigh and shook his head.

Sellier was surprised by his own growing interest in the wildlife Froelicher captured. He admired the bright, lacy butterflies and became fond of a green monkey with a heart-shaped white spot on his nose who always tried to pick his pockets. Out of curiosity he sampled Froelicher's food and later ordered his cook to serve him mangoes and ground-nut soup, but somehow they did not taste so well served on his table.

One day he had a shock. Froelicher had been telling him about the medieval European belief in the relation of the signs of the zodiac and the positions of the planets to the humors of the body, and saying that he thought he had discovered somewhat similar beliefs among the local tribes, when Jenny came up the path carrying Annette's now-battered shoes on her head. She smiled a greeting and sat down at the edge of the clearing to put them on, and as she buckled the familiar-looking straps around her ankles Sellier felt, as clearly as though his hands were there, the resilient texture of her strong legs and the cleft of her buttocks and the warm bristly hump of her pubic mound. His heart filled his chest. Not since his first tour with SCOA had he had an African girl and he could not remember desiring one. When he and Gaux had come to Galoa they had abstained on principle, visiting the army whores in Kankan when they had the chance; and since his marriage to Annette he had, with a few, casual, white exceptions, practiced continence during her absences. Astonished, he watched Jenny stand up and wobble toward them.

His desire did not pass. Each time he saw her—and she was around the village almost every day—he experienced the same sensation of proximate flesh. He looked over other African girls and the European wives and attempted like a schoolboy to conjure up their bodies against his own. But he could not; as much of them as he could materialize was chilly and repellent, while just a memory of Jenny sufficed to stir him.

One night in bed he was imagining her legs tight around his hips, the soar of release...He grunted, sat up, and switched on the light. Enough was enough; she would not make him lose his sleep. He lit a Gauloise, put on his bathrobe and slippers, and walked to his study. To do something, he spread out a contour map and ran his finger along the tracings of possible roads. It occurred to him that he envied Froelicher. A year ago this thought would have seemed so entirely insane that even now he sat back, startled. It was a mad idea. He mentally listed his assets: the business, the bank accounts, his retirement on the Basque coast, for which he owned a plot to build on, Jacques...Annette? Against these he weighed tattered clothes, a mud-walled hut, a tiny income without security of any kind, and Jenny, an ignorant bush girl. Yet the bank accounts were abstract figures, for what pleasure did they provide him? And his mistake in timing the selling of the coffee had given him the feeling that the business controlled him rather than the reverse. No satisfaction in that. Retirement was in the unforseeably far future, Jacques was nearly a stranger, and Annette an expensive pain.

He stubbed his cigarette, distractedly groped for the pack, and lit another. Was he indulging in self-pity? He went over his analysis, seeking a false perception or an oversimplification. His mind repeatedly returned to one striking fact: in Froelicher's life there was joy.

After three days of intermittent meditation, during which the word went around the community to stay clear of the Chief, Sellier planned out a week's work schedule with Daygrand, put him in charge, and went to Conakry on the plane. He spent his days there renewing business acquaintanceships and lobbying for a new road between Kankan and Galoa. A good road to the Kankan railhead would give him an alternative to the Monrovian port facilities and thus a bargaining instrument should he ever need one. Late at night he was invariably a customer at Le Petit Port from which, at closing, a barmaid named Celestine, to whom he had opened wide his wallet, accompanied him to his room at the hotel. She was a rather stupid, greedy girl, and although her shape was pretty her flesh was curiously displeasing, soft almost to flaccidity and spotted with bruises. Nonetheless, on the return plane to Galoa he believed that she had successfully eliminated his state of mind of a week ago.

The following afternoon, rigid with unease, he walked up the path to Froelicher's hut to deliver a butterfly net and a jug of wood alcohol that Froelicher had asked him to buy in Conakry. When he topped the rise Jenny was sweeping the clearing with a broom of bunched twigs. She was doubled from the waist and her torso swayed back and forth as her stiff legs inched forward, extending the semicircle of her sweeping. Rivulets of sweat ran down her cheeks and a drop of saliva glittered at the end of the lemon stick clenched between her teeth. Sellier saw a very ordinary African girl at her chores. His smile was almost as broad as Froelicher's when they shook hands.

"Isn't that a beauty!" Froelicher said, taking the net. "Just this morning I had to give up patching the old one. Perfect timing! I can't thank you enough, Mr. Sellier." They sat down on the two halves of a sundered gasoline drum and Froelicher insisted that Sellier drink some palm wine which Jenny had brought from her village. "Tastes just dreadful, doesn't it? I don't know how I manage to get it down. Well, you're helping." They talked of when the rains would break, and of Conakry. "No, never been there. For you it's a couple of hours in the air. For me, a couple of pairs of shoes maybe."

Sellier had begun to think it time to leave when the white-nosed monkey, who had been swinging and jumping around their legs, leaped to his shoulder, stole his cigarette lighter from the breast pocket of his shirt, and bounded away. Froelicher hooted with laughter as Sellier gave chase, first to the breadfruit tree and then across the clearing toward the path to the stream. There the monkey dodged, and as Sellier changed direction he collided hard with Jenny. She shrieked and stumbled backward, and then rounded her shoulders, cradling one breast in her hands. Froelicher put his arm around her, clucking and peering at her stricken face. Watching them, Sellier's hands weighed her aching breast. Her agony was in his groin.

Celestine had failed her mission.

He decided to treat his absurd desire as a minor ailment; he would walk through it as he would a cold or a boil on his neck. During the weeks that followed, his subordinates diagnosed many illnesses in him. One rumor said that he had gone to Conakry for treatment of his liver, another that he was suffering from low-grade scurvy. A woman from the Midi claimed that his constitution had been depleted by too frequent shower baths. For although he conformed rigidly to his routine, he was often absentminded and his voice had lost its biting growl. Several mornings he appeared unshaven and during one entire day he walked around without his hat.

The fever did not weaken. A second night came when he sat past midnight in his study trying to assess all the factors and to make a new decision. Here he was, he thought, the richest, most powerful man in this part of the world, sick with longing. Why didn't he take what he wanted?

He recalled his and Gaux's pact to have nothing to do with African girls. But that had been made at a time when their position here was tenuous. Trouble with one of the tribes might have forced them to abandon the business. Now it was clear from Froelicher's experience with Jenny that the tribesmen did not object, and in any case the business was unassailably entrenched.

He would be hurting Froelicher of whom he was fond. But Froelicher would not dare attack him and the hurt would surely pass. Froelicher owed him a very great deal.

He would be setting a bad example to the community. To hell with the community, Sellier thought. He put the bread in their mouths and the wealth in their pockets. He would not be intimidated by his subordinates.

It finally seemed to him that not to take Jenny would be an unmanly act.

Intensely excited, he took out a sheet of note paper and wrote to Annette. The weather was terrible, he wrote, and half the community was down with malaria. He had never seen so much of it. He thought it unwise for her and Jacques to come next month, as planned, and suggested that she take a villa in Saint Jean de Luz for the summer. He would try to join them there for a few weeks. He addressed and sealed the letter, went to her closet, and packed one of her brighter dresses in a box.

At the noon break next morning Sellier drove to the hut with the box beside him on the empty seat. If necessary, he was prepared to confront Froelicher and face him down, but luckily he remained unseen.

The clearing was vacant until Sellier called and Jenny stepped out of the hut. At first her face was dumbly startled, then she bowed and smiled uneasily. Sellier, frightened by his ignorance of how to accomplish his purpose, returned her smile. After a few seconds' hesitation he set down the box, opened it, and silently held up the dress. As her expression became eager a knot in his chest liquified. Her hands reached out for the material but he drew it gently back. "You—me." He pointed in turn and then in the direction of the village. "Go to my house. Live there. Then you will have dress. You—me."

He had supposed Froelicher had taught her a limited vocabulary but she seemed baffled, staring gape-mouthed at him. He stepped toward her and pulled her roughly against him. "You—me." And at that the astonishment left her eyes. The lids drooped and she turned her face away from him coyly smiling. "Yes?" He nodded his head toward the village. "Yes?"

She pushed out of his arms and walked several paces away. When she turned there was an unexpected look of shrewdness in her eyes. Then she cast them down and laughed and nodded her head.

Sellier trembled with impatience while she collected her belongings. They made a small bundle in a kerchief but it took fifteen minutes to assemble them. He led the way to the jeep, glancing over his shoulder to be sure she followed. Her skirt prevented her from stepping directly up to the seat and she could not be made to understand the utility of the running board. Finally Sellier leaned over and hauled her in. She held the bucket seat's frame with both hands and uttered shrills of terror at each turning of the road, but when he stopped in front of the bungalow she clapped her hands as though she had witnessed a marvelous feat. Inside she was so enraptured by what she saw that she bumped into walls and tripped on a chair leg.

Sellier's steward Mahfougi, who was waiting to serve lunch, quickly composed his face. He had worked for Sellier twelve years and his discipline was nearly unbreakable.

"Set another place for lunch. She will be living in the back bedroom."

"Yes, sir."

Jenny studied Mahfougi with open curiosity, but when he tried to relieve her of her bundle she clutched it and drew back.

"Tell her you're taking it to her room," Sellier commanded.

Mahfougi spoke to her in dialect and she answered, but Mahfougi reported, "Say she will not give it, sir."

The bundle remained at her side during lunch, which she spent fingering the crockery and tableware, nibbling at the strange food, and watching and sometimes laughing inexplicably at Sellier's and Mahfougi's manners. When Mahfougi offered her the salad bowl she turned in her chair and pressed a finger to one of the brass buttons on his coat. He looked at Sellier for instructions.

"She doesn't want any," Sellier said. But as Mahfougi started toward the kitchen she shrieked and Sellier told him to come back. Jenny clapped her hands and heaped her plate with the salad which, as it turned out, she did not like.

When lunch was over, Sellier took her to his bedroom and they made love. She was not as he had imagined her. Despite her innocence in other matters she was no beginner here. He did not succeed in satisfying her and when he drew away she gave him a glance of reproach, almost entirely masked by pleasure in possession and faith in future possibilities, which was as sophisticated as any Frenchwoman's would have been in similar circumstances. The look amused and shook him.

When he entered the office the clerks glanced up at him a little sharply, a little secretly, he thought, and he wondered whether the word had already been passed.

It hadn't—they were only noticing his flushed cheeks and brightened eyes—but everyone knew next morning. The European women unanimously felt threatened and abused Sellier to their husbands without restraint. "Filthy beast. I always knew there was something rotten in him." "Dirty man. Think of poor Annette." The men wore smiles of self-satisfaction at the spectacle of Sellier's frailty. The event seemed less extraordinary to the Africans, whom Sellier had been surprising for fifteen years with his constructions, gadgets, and improvements. They had never known what to expect. Generally they approved of his taking in Jenny because Annette's comings and goings had always seemed to them unwifely behavior and a bad example to their daughters. Indeed when, as sometimes happened, one of the village girls ran off to Monrovia or Conakry it was said that she was acting like "Madame Chief." That Jenny should move from one man's house to another's did not shock or even surprise them. Since she had attached herself to Froelicher she had been known as "white man's woman," and because no such liaison had ever lasted very long the plural of "man" was expected.

Out of curiosity and an expected sense of triumph, one of the mechanics paid Froelicher a visit the next afternoon. He found him sitting on a drum-half, whittling. "Hello, Froelicher."

"Hello. Come to be treated for something, or just to chat?"

"To chat."

"Sit yourself down." He resumed whittling what looked like the Y of a slingshot.

The mechanic asked, "What do you think of Sellier now?"

"Same as I always did."

"Then you were lying to us about how generous he was, how kind."

"Not a bit. I meant it. I still mean it, every word."

The mechanic hesitated, then said, "Maybe you don't know. He took Jenny. She's over at his place."

"I know."

After a silence the mechanic laughed. "You wanted to get rid of her. I catch on."

"No. I'd be a liar if I didn't admit that I miss her right now. She's a good girl, Jenny. Well." He dropped the knife and the Y and turned to the mechanic. "I'd better explain or you'll think I'm off my head. Right?" The mechanic nodded and Froelicher chuckled. "I thought you would, but hang on. I'm going to pontificate a bit and if it bores you just close your ears and think about payday or something, but this is how I see it. There are certain realities in this world that there's no use trying to change. You can't do it and you're wasting your time if you try. But if you accept them, maybe you can make some good out of them. OK? OK. Now the truth about Sellier is this: he's a powerful man both by his circumstances and by his nature, and it's in his nature to exercise that power. He creates what he wants to create, and he takes what he wants within a set of rules he goes by, and we're all here because of what he's made with that power. Right? Now, if he wanted the girl, and having her wasn't going to break one of his rules, it was in his nature to take her and it's better for us that he has. Better for us that he acts in his natural way. If he started acting differently this whole structure he's built up might disintegrate. It's better for Jenny, too, for everyone. Now, he didn't do this to hurt me. In actual fact, I believe he likes me, and another fact is that he hasn't hurt me much. Oh, I miss the girl but I won't have any trouble finding another—one boy was around this morning suggesting I take his sister, and if she won't do there'll be others. Anyway, there always have been. And on the other side of the balance from my little loss, or inconvenience you might say, look what he does for me. He provides my house; he builds an airfield and a post office which make it possible for me to get my specimens alive to Europe; he puts money in my pocket by appointing me medical man. He's used his power for me in all those ways and if it weren't for him I couldn't live here in a country which, for me, is paradise. On balance, I think he looks mighty good."

The mechanic left, shaking his head.

When Sellier opened his front door that evening he heard laughter, Mahfougi's and the cook's, from the rear of the house. In the living room he found Jenny squatting on her haunches and clearly sulking; she shoved his hand away and wouldn't look at him. He continued through to the kitchen and surprised them. "Something's funny," he said in his hardest voice.

"No, sir," Mahfougi said.

"I heard you laughing from the front door."

"Cook and I make joke." He busied himself at the sink until Sellier firmly gripped his arm.

"What was funny?"

Mahfougi glanced at the cook who was bending over the provisions locker, then fearfully at Sellier. "That woman, sir, does not know how to use bathroom. Go out in bush there, behind house."

Both Jenny and Mahfougi being Africans, Sellier very nearly commanded him to teach her the bathroom's mechanisms. Only in the split second before he spoke did their difference in sex occur to him. He grunted, returned to the living room, and led Jenny to the bathroom.

The lesson was charming and hilarious. She jumped back when he turned on the faucets and had to hold his hand in the stream for a minute before she dared to do so. As he adjusted the temperature from cold to hot she gasped in amazement. Then he demonstrated the shower, making motions of soaping himself at which she laughed heartily. And the toilet was even funnier until the flush, which truly delighted her. She wanted to pull the chain again and again and he had to restrain her hand until the reservoir filled. Apparently the rushing water pleased her eye.

At dinner she treated Mahfougi with theatrical disdain, pushing away the dishes he offered rather than speak to him. This began the trouble between them. Everything in the house excited her curiosity, and since she had nothing to do all day she did her best to satisfy it. Each piece of material was fingered time and again, each object handled and disarranged. She went through all the drawers and carelessly left them open and their contents scattered elsewhere. Her particular fascination was Annette's clothes which Mahfougi had been taught to fold, align, and hang with rigid neatness. He obviously resented straightening up after her.

Two weeks after Jenny's seduction Sellier had a stroke of loneliness. His subordinates were sufficiently cowed not to smile at him or make insinuations, but in their eyes was a glint of recognition, of pretended equality, or even superiority which forced him to be harder and more distant than ever before. Jenny satisfied him sexually but they could not talk. He decided to make his peace with Froelicher. He would not ask forgiveness;

he would not apologize or demean himself in any way; he would simply go there as he had in the past and speak of their usual topics, and Froelicher would have to accept that the situation as it stood was final. What else could he do?

Froelicher's greeting was as warm as ever. "I've got something new to show you. I caught a butterfly this morning I've never seen before—haven't even had time to look it up." He ducked into the hut and reappeared with a board on which the butterfly was pinned. "See how the wing spots look like orange eyes? I've been trying to imagine what in nature they might resemble and I can't think of anything." After Sellier had looked for a minute Froelicher said, "That's enough wildlife, I guess. How are you? Jenny treating you all right?"

"All right."

"Glad to hear it. Tell her from me she'd better, if you've invented some kind of language. Tell you the truth, though, you don't look just right. Not feeling well?"

"I'm very well," Sellier said, and saw a girl walking up the path from the stream with laundry in her arms. For a moment he thought his mind had gone but then he saw that it wasn't Jenny. This one was a little shorter with a wider, rather square face, big eyes above a flat but delicately shaped nose. When she dropped the wet clothes he saw that she was naked to the waist.

"Hello, Sadie," Froelicher called and waved, and she gave him that smile that it seemed only he could produce. "I call this one Sadie," he said to Sellier. "Didn't take me long, did it? Ah, I'm a devil in Galoa, all right." They silently watched her hang the clothes until he added, "Look at those little breasts. I'd like to go right over there and bite them."

Sellier sensed their taut brown skin against his lips. Not again, he thought, not already, but each gesture she made confirmed her body to him.

"But you know," Froelicher went on, "she seems so unconscious of them I hardly dare touch. I think I might shock her if I did. Think she'd be shocked, Mr. Sellier?"

"You're the expert."

At the bungalow Sellier found Jenny sprawled on the living-room couch. Lipstick was smeared unevenly on her mouth and

Annette's dress was askew across her body. She looked both whorish and silly.

But Sellier became ever more strongly attached to her. He recognized that she was growing sulkier, more demanding, more arrogant with Mahfougi, that in fact she was fast losing the purity that had charmed him. But instead of revolting him and making him wish her gone, her apparent dissatisfaction drove him all the harder to content her. This urge to make her happy and well behaved had little to do with Jenny as she was or with his specific feelings toward her. All his adult life had been spent making unpromising situations come right; to do so had become a habit of mind. He had signed his first contract with SCOA after failing his second baccalaureate examination. He had turned that failure to account by learning the business and rising in the SCOA organization. The war had brought business to a halt but he had seized on that setback as the occasion to go out on his own. In Galoa he had triumphed over ignorance, suspicion, and lethargy in country that was far from the richest of West Africa. Each improvement had seemed nearly impossible at its conception and his major stroke—getting the Liberians to build a road from Monrovia—a wild dream. Yet he had accomplished it all by meticulousness, by craft, and by the skillful handling of his underlings.

Only Annette had remained outside this pattern. Perhaps because she had never loved him he had felt it beyond his power to affect her person. Or perhaps it was simply that since he could not feel responsible for her during her prolonged absences all sense of responsibility toward her had dried up. But Jenny, dependent, unpromising in her ignorance and selfishness, aroused his will. His self-respect had become involved in her evolution to a contented, proper mistress.

To relieve her daytime boredom he taught her how to use the radio and gramophone and to play the game of darts. He demonstrated table manners and showed her how Annette's clothes should be worn, and got her a sewing machine and blots of cloth on which to practice its operation. Her ineptness as a pupil was a whip to his persistence.

Mahfougi's irritation with her became increasingly plain. They occasionally exchanged hot words which Mahfougi would sullenly translate, or mistranslate, to Sellier. According to Mahfougi the disputes invariably concerned objects misplaced or dirtied or broken. Then one evening Sellier was astonished to hear them laughing together in another room. Was their enmity for show, he wondered? Did they, while he was out— Would he now be jealous of *Mahfougi*?

One day at the end of a translation Mahfougi added, "Be no-good woman, sir. Bring nothing but trouble to house."

Sellier fired him and in two weeks the cook had left too. At first he considered the possibility of having Jenny do the work. But she had not come here to keep house; he felt quite certain he would lose her if he insisted on it, and that in case of her acceptance the work would be badly done. He hired the first cook and steward who presented themselves. They lasted ten days, and again it was a question of the "woman." Jenny had learned to command them, to demand tea and Coca Cola, for which she had developed a passion. This time Sellier consulted Froelicher who rounded up two boys from Jenny's village. Being tribal brothers they would not molest her and it seemed likely she would get on well with them.

Socially, indeed, this move was a complete success. The house often rang with laughter. The drawbacks were that the cook's dishes were barely edible—he had once worked briefly as a kitchen boy for an Englishman in Freetown—and that the steward knew only the rudiments of housekeeping. Sellier could teach the cook nothing, knowing nothing himself. He instructed the steward in how to serve at table and how to make a bed, but there was much he couldn't teach him—the amount of bleach which should be added to a tub of clothes, for instance, and the use of a hot iron. Soon he was wearing unbleached, unpressed clothes which were not even strictly clean.

The vases in the living room stood empty collecting dust, and the chairs and tables, moved back and forth when the floor was swept, were left at odd angles to one another until the room had lost all intelligible design. Sellier rearranged the furniture several times but within a few days the confusion had returned. To avoid annoyance, he decided not to notice. As the weeks passed other things went purposely unnoticed and each new act of blindness increased both his loneliness and an aggressive determination to change nothing on account of it. He contended with disapproving inner voices, Annette's sometimes where the house was concerned, at business a sarcastic voice which echoed the townspeople's ill-concealed mockery. His own former attitudes were speaking. The more critical these voices became, the harder became his defenses against them. His clothes were unpressed? He walked through the day without a glance at them. He could no longer invite Daygrand and his wife to what had been a weekly dinner? He avoided obligating himself by refusing all invitations. But each action of this kind demanded fresh strength, for with each unexpected gesture he was breaking what amounted to tradition. The routines of living sapped his vitality as they never had before.

One night, sitting late over the August balance sheet, he was interrupted by a crash of glass in the kitchen. He raised his eyes and saw a lizard on the inside of the screen. It was one of the small, pinkish, semitransparent kind and it was stalking a moth which was preening its wings some inches away. Beyond the moth was another bug, and files speckled the circle of lamplight on the ceiling. Sellier pinched the bridge of his nose and closed his eyes, but the expected anger and disgust did not possess him. Instead, it was as though a heavy wave, cooling and depressing, had broken over him. He let himself sink under it, limp against the chair, his breathing so shallow it seemed nearly to have stopped. He rested there against a bottom—*the* bottom, he believed, the ultimate perversion of his wishes. Then his gorge slowly rose. He sat up and turned off the light. From now on there could be nothing but improvement. Jenny and the boys would learn his ways, would learn to please him. But as he thought of all the routines and awarenesses he would have to teach them a fresh wave fell on his shoulders. He left the study, mixed a drink, listened for a while to the undulating music of the shortwave radio, and went gloomily to bed.

Several evenings later Froelicher paid Sellier an unexpected visit. He knocked at the door and when Jenny opened it they exchanged smiles and bows. "How are you, old girl? My what finery! Still don't understand a word I say? Of course not."

He came into the living room peering about as though the place were strange. "Things have sort of gone to seed here, haven't they? How are you, Mr. Sellier? You don't look so good either."

"Like a drink, Froelicher?"

"Just what I need, I guess. I want a little Dutch courage. Dear me, look at that." He ran his fingers over a tabletop rutted by glass rings. "Dear me."

Sellier handed him a Scotch and they sat down while Jenny stood in the doorway watching them.

"Well, Mr. Sellier, I'm not going to pretend this is a social call. I came to say something and I'll try to get straight to the point." He paused, appeared to gulp, and then noticing his drink, swallowed half of it. When he looked up at Sellier his mouth was open to speak, but he interrupted himself by saying, "Maybe one of Sadie's soups would do you good. Clean you right out, clean as a whistle." Sellier smiled.

"But I didn't come to say that, and anyway the lower intestine is a simple business. What I came to say is this: Mr. Sellier, there are a number of queer people in this world." He hesitated and gulped again. "And I'm one of them." To Sellier's grunt he added, "You won't argue that, Mr. Sellier. Nobody would. I'm a pretty queer fish and I know it, and if anyone thinks differently they're not thinking right. I'm what they call an eccentric and a lot of other words not so pretty. Now. Here comes the part you aren't going to like, Mr. Sellier. You're going to say to yourself, who does this little fellow think he is, telling me about myself? But on the other hand I'm going to tell you something nice. Mr. Sellier, you aren't an eccentric. You're a strong, normal, conventional man." Froelicher laughed suddenly. "Right? Am I right?"

Sellier nodded. "So?"

"So. I'm a happy man. I have everything I need. I have a life that suits me fine, but it wouldn't suit you, now would it?"

Sellier waited while Froelicher sipped his drink.

"I know it wouldn't because we're different kinds of men. Sadie's soup might help your intestines but that's about the only point we have in common. Now, here's the hard part. When you brought Jenny over here—now don't get excited, this isn't bad—I said to myself, good. If Mr. Sellier wants the girl he should take her, because it's Mr. Sellier's habit to get what he wants and if he doesn't he might get sick or something and we'd all be in trouble. That's what I thought then, but I've changed my mind. Jenny's making you sick. I imagine you had some misunderstanding with your wife"—Sellier stood up and Froelicher speeded his voice, getting up from his chair—"and thought maybe Jenny could heal some kind of pain inside you. But she can't, Mr. Sellier, she's just going to make things worse."

Sellier, stony faced, started walking toward the door and Froelicher followed. "Don't think that I want Jenny back—it isn't that. But you're an important man and you've got to act like one whether you like it or not. I guess you don't like it right now, but that's just too bad. Get rid of Jenny, get your cook and steward back, and if you don't like your wife any more, get another one— but the same kind. It's the only kind for you."

Sellier opened the door for him and Froelicher continued talking from the stoop even after Sellier had closed the door between them. "There's only one way for you to live, Mr. Sellier. You've got to deny yourself. You can't mix the two things up."

Jenny stared at Sellier as he came through the living-room door, at once mystified and proud of the forcefulness with which he had treated Froelicher. Enraged and insulted, he could not look at her. That Froelicher, of all people, should add his voice to those of his enemies! That this man he had befriended and provided for should dare to comment on his relation to Annette! That he should feel competent to explain Sellier to himself and give advice! Pacing the floor, he lapsed into a recapitulation of Froelicher's treason.

Everyone remarked on the abrupt change in Froelicher's temper. His smile had vanished and in its place was a faint compression of the lips, as though he had tasted something bitter. People speculated on the reasons for his frequent and public attempts to talk to Sellier. He would be loitering near the office at noon or watching near the bungalow at nightfall. The Chief brushed by him every time. Froelicher lost weight and his eyes hollowed. A day came when one of the men asked him, "What happened to your paradise?"

He laughed at that, but off-key and too long. "I guess it's still there," he said. "Right under my nose."

By now Jenny was wearing Annette's entire Galoa wardrobe in her walks around town. For one Frenchwoman this was the necessary goad to action. She wrote a letter to Annette describing the current situation, signed it "A friend," and rather than risk it being noticed at the post office gave it to her trucker husband to mail in Monrovia. He waited patiently in the line before the stamp window for fifteen minutes and then, with only two customers ahead of him, tore up the letter. He told himself that he had done this out of a sense of loyalty to Sellier. Why should he spoil his fun? But in fact, like the other men in town, he was enjoying Sellier's comedown too much to want to arrest it. Had they thought about it they might have worried that the change in him might affect their livelihoods. But the sight of this man whose standards had once been so rigidly demanding, whose will had been so inflexibly ambitious, relaxing all for the sake of an ignorant bush girl pleased their hearts. His fall was a repayment to them for all the harsh orders, humiliations, and sharp verbal prods to which they had been treated.

It was not long before Annette knew. Everyone worthy of a confidence in the colony was aware of Jenny's presence in the Sellier household; it had been only a question of time before a woman wanting to gloat a bit on the misfortune of the heretofore overprivileged Madame Sellier, or simply to share her own disgust with men, would inform the injured wife. In the last week of September, Sellier received a telegram from Annette saying that she would arrive the following Friday. He wired back that the visit was inadvisable. Malaria was still prevalent and there were cases of blackwater fever. Her answer was succinct, "Arriving Friday fifth," and Sellier felt certain of her knowledge.

Froelicher responded immediately to Sellier's reluctant demand for help. Together they convinced Jenny she would be happy in Conakry for a few weeks, indeed that she would be queen on the money Sellier would send her until she could return. At first she was suspicious and lay kicking and crying on her bed, but when the sums were translated into garments and Coca Colas she became quieter and finally nodded her agreement. When she left the house, the one small bundle with which she had arrived had become three fat bundles of plunder. Watching her go, Sellier deeply felt his failure.

Assured that Jenny had left, Mahfougi agreed to return at higher wages. The cook had vanished but a replacement was found and he and Mahfougi set to work with DDT, soap, and polish to repair the damages. The town was much amused by these urgent changes, and for different reasons Froelicher became high-spirited too. Rather than Sellier's lieutenant in the operation he seemed its prime mover. He not only made the suggestions, but saw that they were carried out. He shared Mahfougi's work, rid the house of lizards with his net, and engaged a seamstress to make new shirts and shorts to replace Sellier's discolored ones. Early every morning he appeared at Sellier's breakfast table and after a brief conference would say, "Now get out of here, Mr. Sellier, and go to your business. We've got work to do." Sellier went.

The pair drove out together to meet Annette's plane. While Sellier sat waiting behind the wheel, impeccable, a shine on the straps of his sandals, a new hat, face freshly shaved and powdered, Froelicher jittered about talking to one or another in the crowd, returning to say a few words to Sellier, and scanning the sky. "The mother of the bride," one man remarked.

It had not occurred to anyone that once Sellier was clean and neat again he would look differently than he had six months before, but seeing him now in his familiar pose Froelicher and others noticed more than superficial changes. The line of his jaw had lost its lean edge and around his eyes the skin was softly puffed, not in sacs of fatigue but in unhealthy-looking cushions. Most striking was his posture: his shoulders appeared to have rounded and his head lolled back on his neck. One no longer sensed rigidity.

The plane circled and came in. The drums exploded and at the end of the runway the Dakota turned and taxied toward the jeep, blowing red clouds of dust into the forest. Froelicher retreated into the crowd while Sellier waited by the wheel chocks. The motors were cut, the ramp fitted, and the door opened from inside. Annette stepped into the aperture, formidably neat in blue shantung, inscrutable behind dark glasses. She paused there a second, neither gesturing nor speaking to her husband standing directly below her. Then she stepped down and Gaux appeared behind her. He smiled at his former partner and waved his hand. Stupefied, Sellier studied the sleekness of Gaux's head and the clearness of his complexion and the sharp cut of his suit. He had lost so much weight he resembled the man Sellier had first known. Sellier was so intent that he barely heard Annette's "Well, the pig!" halfway down the ladder. The other Europeans hid their smirks.

The conversation was sparse and trivial on the trip back to the house. Whatever they had come to say, Sellier would not help them with it. They went to their rooms and he returned to the office and remained there until closing time. During dinner their attack began. First they brought up the price he had accepted for the coffee, pointing to it as evidence of his illness. Then they nagged him on the lagging projects of the summer months. To Sellier's surprise and embarrassment, and their satisfaction, he had to call on Daygrand to explain exactly where certain matters stood. Gaux relished his revenge. "We all understand, old friend. It happens to the best of us. This wretched climate..." words Sellier had said to Gaux not so long ago which were repeated now with an insinuating smile. Annette, of course, saw the whole affair in the light of her injured dignity. "Who will do business with a degenerate? In any case, I certainly will never live here again and be the laughing stock of the colony."

The *bonne petite bourgeoise*! "You, the model wife," Sellier growled.

"I've done nothing to disgrace Jacques. Nothing!"

Discretion, to her the sole essential virtue. If he had had a discreet affair with a respectable white woman, the governor general's wife, say, she might even have felt proud of him. Gaux looked amused. No doubt he had encouraged her conventional sense of propriety.

Sellier said, "You've done nothing for Jacques, either, except to introduce him to your string of Jules."

"Pig!" Then she said calmly, "Stay here. We'll divorce. I've already seen a lawyer and I have the witnesses. You'll never see Jacques again; you'll only pay our bills."

"You'd like that, wouldn't you?"

She shrugged and turned away.

During the three days the battle lasted Froelicher lingered near the bungalow seeking scraps of information on its progress. Sadie, wide-eyed and silent, was usually near him.

Sellier's argument was gradually reduced to a point on which he was absolutely certain—that if the business were left in the hands of a caretaker it would stagnate. Only the owners could exercise the initiative necessary to expansion and prosperity. But his antagonists were so blinded by their bitterness that they would not agree. Annette said, "Do you imagine you're the only man alive capable of running this?" And Gaux said, mildly enough, "Daygrand seems a good man," but smiling with the knowledge that in implying Daygrand would do a better job than Sellier he was delivering a cutting insult.

Finally Sellier agreed to leave on condition that Gaux remain in charge until he was well enough to return—for by now they had pried into his mind a tacit admission that he was ill. Gaux replied that he could not, that he owned half a vineyard now and managed a string of three service stations in the Bordeaux area; he could not be absent long. And Sellier understood that this, too, was a part of Gaux's revenge—that like him, Sellier would have to start fresh in the business world.

"We worked fifteen years here," Sellier said, "and you want it to go for nothing."

"Perhaps you'll enjoy retirement," said Gaux. "I do."

They proposed that he make over to Daygrand twenty percent of his stock, to be paid for piecemeal out of salary, and that Daygrand be put in sole charge. Sellier saw precisely what this would mean. Daygrand was a born lieutenant: meticulous, prompt, conscientious, and, if not given orders, very indecisive. He would find a hundred reasons against any new project. The routine operations would inevitably falter because he could not improvise. Sellier repeated these facts and repeated them until Gaux and Annette began to treat him as a maniac. "I *believe* we've heard that," "*Very* interesting," as though his words had no pertinence to the situation!

Late on their third night of talks Sellier started to speak and faltered. His mouth closed and the saliva tasted bitter in it; the words and facts that flashed across his mind seemed useless and discredited. They were impossible to communicate; there was no new way to state them. For a minute he sat in silence, hearing his antagonists' voices but not what they said, teetering in balance between tenacious pride on one side and hatred and discouragement on the other. Then he thought, *it will serve them right.* He nodded and said, "All right. Finished." In the surprised silence, he shouted. "You idiots do the work for a change! You make the decisions! You take care of the future! See how well you do with it. You take care of me!" Gaux arranged a controlled little smile; Annette looked slackly stupid. "You'll pay, you'll pay," he glared at them in turn. "You'll get what you wanted and you'll pay for it. Write an agreement, Gaux." He sat staring at the floor, supreme in his vindictiveness, while Gaux typed it out.

Mahfougi was roused from bed to witness Sellier's signature. He entered the room sleepily but was immediately and uneasily wide-eyed, looking from one face to another. "The meek shall inherit the earth," Sellier said. "Because I say so."

During the four days they waited for the plane Sellier brooded in his study. Gaux took care of all the details and got a *notaire* down from Kankan to draw up the contract. Sellier was both amused and dismayed by the clauses inserted at Daygrand's insistence. The exact number of days of leave per year, his right to occupy Sellier's bungalow, his right to the title of *seul maitre*—as though any of the men would think of him as such simply because it was written in the contract! How like the man! A new second-in-command would be sent from Paris; clearly Daygrand felt that his current familiarity with the others would be detrimental in his new position unless he was recessed from them by a new intermediary. He had the unrescindable right to fire personnel and this meant that the fugitives would go, for he had always been scared of them, and probably Froelicher of whom he was suspicious. Lastly, there was a lengthy paragraph whose object was to insure that neither Gaux nor Sellier could attempt to control the workings of the business through another employee. He mistrusted his own strength to that extent!

Sellier pictured Galoa's future very clearly. Daygrand would try to run it by conventional bureaucratic rules. The cost of administration would rise sharply and the pettyfogging would result in corners cut, in subtle thievery, in a sluggish attitude among the men, and distrust among the Africans which would make the business increasingly difficult to operate. Risk-taking competitors would move in and the area would be cut up. The business would ossify—Daygrand finding a thousand reasons why it was not his fault that it had—and be sold off.

Sellier viewed this prospect with increasing regret and pain. To cheer himself he remembered that he would still draw income from the business and that he had plenty of capital to start a new venture. But as the hours passed it became ever clearer to him that it was not the loss of revenue which caused his regret at leaving, nor had it been the actual revenue that had kept him so hard at work for fifteen years. He thought of the fugitives whom he had enabled to live normal lives, of Froelicher for whom he had furnished a paradise, of the Africans whose standard of life and health he had radically changed. He thought of the school and of the neatly arranged mechanical facilities of the town, the water supply, and the airfield. And it seemed to him that the bank balances and the produce broker's credit figures which he had known by heart had satisfied him because they were symbols of his creation and his responsibility. Separated from their source the figures themselves were small consolation. What would become of these people? What would become of Jenny?

There was a knock at the door the afternoon before they were to leave. Sellier heard Annette walk to it and say coldly, "Well?"

Froelicher's voice said, "I'd like to see Mr. Sellier, if I may."

"Get away from here," Annette said. "You're the cause of all the trouble."

"You're right, Mrs. Sellier. That's what I came to tell him. I'm trouble wherever I go. I take it as it comes, from day to day. It's my nature. Other people get used to thinking they can too." He shook his head. "You understand."

"I've told him where the trouble was," she said, "and I'll tell him you've admitted it. Now get along."

Sellier sat still, wanting no more arguments. It was neither his nor Froelicher's fault—whatever *it* was. In jealousy and revenge Annette and Gaux had seized a pretext to remove him from his work and he had ceded in a moment of rage. That was all.

Next morning Sellier shaved and dressed with unusual care, put on his hat, and walked about the town shaking hands and saying good-bye. He was determined to show no trace of sorrow or defeat and the stiffness of his bearing and severity of his voice strangely touched the people, recalling as it did years of joint effort. They uttered their good-byes feeling a measure of guilt for his downfall; they were suddenly aware of what they owed him and were afraid. Only the fugitives dared sympathy, an act of generosity since they knew that his leaving endangered them. Crespin said, "Don't let them pull you to pieces, Chief," and others, "You'll be back." Sellier did not answer but they knew he understood.

As usual, he sat waiting for the plane in the jeep's driver's seat. Africans crowded around the car and stepped up singly to shake his hand. The Liberian Consul had prepared a farewell speech: "I desire to tender your best wishes on behalf of this body and body of Liberian nation." Sellier joked with them and slapped their shoulders while Annette and Gaux talked together or stared straight ahead. But when the propellers had stilled and the ramp had been put in place and the door opened and there were only a hundred feet for him to walk before it all was gone and finished, a lump formed in his windpipe and his vision blurred. He got out of the jeep and turned his head this way and that at the run-together green of the forest and the bright colors of the Africans' clothes and the red earth of the strip. Gaux touched him lightly on the arm and they started walking three abreast. After a few steps a strange sound, applause, broke out and steadily persisted. Halfway to the plane a figure jumped in front of them. Gaux tried to brush him aside but Froelicher said, "I'm to blame, Mr. Sellier. Don't blame yourself. I caused the trouble."

"No, no," Sellier said. "Don't think that." During a second that his eyes were clear he saw that Froelicher's were streaming tears.

"Yes. I know it. I'm trouble wherever I go. I know it."

"I tell you, no," said Sellier. "You were my friend."

"You don't know how bad a one."

Their hands met and clasped, then Froelicher stepped out of the way.

The crowd solemnly applauded until the door was shut, and waved hands as the plane took off.

Two days later, having lost his protector, Froelicher moved on.

BAKTI'S HAND

B akti's briefcase was heavy in his hand but he did not glance
at the cars passing in his direction. He stamped along the
muddy kilometer from his barren apartment to the university's
gate watching ahead to avoid the puddles, looking across the flat
fields at the olive-oil factory with its now abandoned stork's next
still perched on its shorter chimney, and at the shepherds, hidden
under the hoods of their *djellabahs*, tending their dirty flocks.
No disgrace not to own a car in socialist Algeria, yet he did not
want to see a colleague's brake lights and be forced to trot over
and accept the lift. Any of his colleagues—Algerian, French, or
the solitary American, Sledd, whose largest, newest model
Mercedes was something of a shock. Most especially Bakti did
not want to see Benslimane who was chauffeuring the
distinguished visitor from Lyons, Le Professeur Carrere, Docteur
d'Etat, on the highest rung of the French academic ladder.

Bakti need not have been concerned. He reached the gate a
few minutes before nine, the appointed hour, but no Oran faculty

meeting had ever begun within a half hour of schedule. As the gatekeeper, whose face had been crushed by shrapnel around the left eye, opened the grill for him, Bakti could see through the lines of palms that there were no cars parked by the Faculte des Lettres.

He opened the conference room and by putting the two tables together to make one, aligning the metal folding chairs around it, and straightening the few stacks of supplies in the shelves, made it look as formal as possible. The campus had been a French aviation base, built in a colonial "moorish" style with high ceilings and tall windows, so that formality was both natural to it and absurd. Given the tininess of the furniture, the bad light and the flaking of the gray wall paint, not much could be done. Bakti went outside and smoked a cigarette, sitting on a bench near the doors of the audi-torium that had been a mess hall. It was very quiet. The examinations had been given ten days before and most of the students had vanished to return on the day the results would be announced. In the distance he could hear a solitary light plane taking off, circling and coming down, then taking off again.

His colleagues arrived separately, the first one eighteen minutes late. They were apologetic to Bakti for their tardiness, and courteous, each in his own way. The French teachers of Spanish bowed slightly as they shook hands. Mlle. Arnaud, young and radical, briefly surrendered the ends of her fingers. The stout Englishwoman, married to an Algerian engineer, forgot to extend her hand and blushed. Sledd neither offered his hand nor blushed, but drawled out *"Bonjour,"* making two words of it. Aidouni was jumpy with correctness, as finally was Benslimane, the other French-university-trained Algerian. All of them were overshadowed in graciousness by Professor Carrere who was extremely happy to be among them, cocking his cameo head this way and that and savoring the introductions. His pink cheeks gave off a sharp cologne, while his blazer, hard white collar, and the green and white striped ribbon in his buttonhole radiated those reasons for which he had been imported for a few days at such expense to the government—his unquestionable qualifications, his eminently sound judgment. To Bakti's surprise he and Carrere were equally short, but they weighed quite differently on the earth.

Bakti led the way inside. They seated themselves, and Bakti standing, eyes on the table, said a few words about procedure. During this meeting they would arrive at final grades for all the upperclassmen taking certificates in English and Spanish. Since there were so few in Spanish they would be dealt with first, but the Spanish faculty was asked not to leave when their section had been completed. It was hoped that today with the collaboration of Professor Carrere precedents could be set for the judgment of all the language sections in future. For this reason the Arabic section, Benslimane and Aidouni, was present, although no certificates would be offered in Arabic until next year.

Bakti took his seat and the "Spaniards" got quickly to their business, a formality, for they had had only four students and had certainly made their decisions in advance. Carrere followed their dialogue alertly but did not speak. Because he was a Professor of English rather than of Spanish? Because the two "Spaniards" were French? When three students had been passed and the fourth invited to take a remedial exam in October, Bakti asked for comments. There were none. "Mlle. Arnaud, will you please begin with the first candidate in English."

"Benabadji, Abdelkader, 8.4 in Translation." And the name went around the table. He had achieved 6.8 in British History and Institutions, 11.8, his high, in American Literature. Bakti had given him 10.0, the passing grade, in his course in American Civilization. Having announced it and then, like the others, having averaged Benabadji's failing score, he glanced up along the table and waited for Carrere's approval. Carrere gave it, faintly and gravely nodding his head, and Bakti ducked down to his grades-ledger in sudden embarrassment. His colleagues all knew how bitterly he had opposed the invitation to Carrere, that he had offered his resignation when the dean had overruled him. The Department of Languages did not need an antique from Lyons to legitimize its degrees! he had protested, and they must all have heard him say it. Bakti the party member, the committed revolutionary! So that now it must seem that he was playing *petit negre*.

Bakti hunched his shoulders, feeling the uneasiness around him, no help to his own discomfort. How had he so wrongly calculated? When a prisoner of the French twelve years ago, his tactful discretion had not saved him from torture—his left hand now holding the grades-ledger was scarred on its back where one electrode had been implanted. But after stubbornness and terror of his own comrades had combined to keep his mouth shut until fainting, deference had freed him of suspicion. He had supposed, since he had been welcomed out the prison doors by the triumphant FLN while the French were scrambling for the boats, that now Carrere would take his deference as irony, an irony which would act as a cement between himself and the others. But Carrere evidently sensed no irony. He indeed seemed ready to be helpful to a teacher so lacking in authority!

"Perhaps," Carrere was saying, "I might facilitate matters by averaging the grades as they are read out?" And not waiting for an answer he took a fat pen from an inside pocket and a sheet of paper from Benslimane's notebook. Then he looked gravely around the table; he was at their service.

Bakti nodded to Mlle. Arnaud that she should start the second round. She glared at him a moment, then putting her elbows on the table and joining her hands under her chin, her ultimate in dignified gestures, she read off, "Benmiloud, Mohammed, 7.8 in Translation."

Since Carrere was dutifully recording the numbers, acting like the secretary that the department could not afford, it should have been possible to forget his position and potential power, to think of him simply as a functionary in a routine. On the contrary his unique elevation was emphasized. That a *docteur d'etat* should be doing clerical work for such a crew of people! Bakti glanced at Mlle. Arnaud, so prim and icy, and saw the sad little brownish stone in the ring on her little finger and the plainness of her blouse and sweater, and they made him feel the tremors in the shaky table and the dankness of the walls around them. Images of a conference room at Leeds—masked fluorescent lights, a solid blond wood table with ashtrays the size of soup bowls for English pipe smokers, and notepaper laid meticulously before each seat—crossed his mind. And then the industrial-looking campus of New York State University at Fredonia, not pretty because there was so much equipment—laboratories, gymnasiums, auditoriums—that the exteriors of the buildings were ungainly, like dustcovers over office machines. Why hadn't they sent him to some poorer, gloomier places for study outside Algeria?

Now Carrere was saying, "Why don't we average the first two essays and then the first midterm...?"

And Bakti found himself saying that yes, that sounded to be a very good idea, let's do it that way, not consulting the others. He turned crisply on them, prompting scores and demanding repetitions, and their expressions changed. Sledd cocked his head a bit quizzically; the Englishwoman's upper lip beaded; Benslimane's mouth had gone disparagingly slack. Never mind; Bakti had got himself back in hand and working, and he saw that the lids of Carrere's eyes had raised. Carrere's voice had a new, clearer tone. Together they would be able to get the work done now, without a lot of unnecessary sensitivity. Carrere was a professional, so was he, and they needed to understand no more than that about one another.

"—At Lyons it is our habit to give extra weight to the second essay, on the ground, needless to say, that improvement should be recognized and rewarded."

What could Bakti do but agree to the principle involved?

"In general in the department at Lyons we find..."

No doubt it was so found everywhere.

"At Leeds...," said Bakti *a propos* a student's being unable to take an examination and unavailable for its makeup. Carrere's lids came slowly down as Bakti painstakingly explained the Leeds formula. Of course, Bakti realized in mid-development, only French procedures would count for Carrere. He reached the end of the outline and brief pros and cons and looked coolly at Carrere for comment. None came. "The Leeds formula seems fair enough to me," Bakti said, looking elsewhere around the table.

Carrere's silence had released them and several wished to talk, but Carrere cut them off by a clearing of his throat. "At Lyons—" he began. What Bakti had wished to believe was a common professionalism had simply been an aspect of the old colonial game. Let the cooperative Algerian speak first to make way for the colonial fiat! Bakti had ignored and silenced the colleagues with whom his entire future lay! O smart Bakti, shrewd, double-thinking fellow! He ground the blunt end of his ballpoint against the table top and a zinging vibration made Carrere's lids flutter and his glance shoot down. Bakti stopped his hand and glared at it. He had been a fellow professional in Carrere's eyes until the moment he had had something to contribute. How could he have imagined that Carrere would want to find the best solution, rather than the one he could impose! Bakti, idiot!

It seemed that at Lyons there were some half dozen categories of acceptable excuses for missing an examination, all of them *verified*, attested to by competent authorities which equally, of course, did not exist in Algeria and would not exist for a generation to come. "This has the advantage, needless to say...on the whole it seems satisfactory to all concerned." Carrere's complicated and monotone discourse had softened the others to doughy speechlessness. The spectacle of their unsettled mouths put the lash to Bakti.

"Professor Carrere, we do not have those agencies here, those means of supervision. Our situation is quite different, and I am sure you will understand that we are looking for an Algerian solution, that we cannot borrow our solutions any longer from abroad..." The absolute hush pleased him; so did Carrere's eyes.

Carrere said, "If you do not want to know what I know of such matters, I wonder why you asked me here?"

"We are happy to have your advice, but we are anxious to find an Algerian solution."

Benslimane rushed to rescue the moment. "We were extremely gratified that you could accept our invitation, Monsieur le Professeur. While Bakti is quite right in saying we seek an Algerian solution, these solutions must of course be made up of others antecedent to our own. It is precisely for this reason..." And this was worse than *petit negre*. Benslimane, Bakti's equal as head of the Arabic section; Benslimane, a leader of the Cadets of the Revolution! Apparently his wish was to gloss things over until there would seem to have been no conflict at all! His eyes darted around the table as he spoke and he was watched in silence. When he had finished, Carrere could be gracious again.

"I feel quite certain, my dear friends, that we can resolve our problems with patience, with mutual understanding. Certainly there is no necessity for comment on the sad political history between our two nations; I feel we would do well to ignore politics, that politics can only be disruptive to deliberations on strictly academic matters."

And Bakti could see he was getting away with this, that the others would now prefer to remove politics from the room, that is to say, remove Bakti's anger, and they would happily ignore the fact that it was Carrere who had been playing politics and so cleverly that he had produced the classic colonial situation: the colonized split and angry at one another while the colonial power coasts on serenely to its goals. Of course they would be happy enough to forget contentious politics! Bakti raised his left hand against his chest and turned the back of it toward Benslimane who appeared so mistily pleased by Carrere's reaction that he could see nothing. Benslimane knew the scar's significance, after all!

You despicable winner, Carrere! Bakti could see him walking immaculately through the cold rains of Lyons. His trousers would never lose their press, the collar of his raincoat would never wrinkle. Nothing a student could say or do would surprise him. Their names would be dots on a list, their faces shapes in a mass—except the pretty ones. Carrere had an eye for those all right, had an eye for Mlle. Arnaud right here at the table, and probably could have her. Would, quite likely. He would fix her with those pale eyes under the arched brows, never smiling, never being ingratiating or apparently trying to charm, and talk about her future when she returned to teach in France. Where had she in mind to teach? Ah, perhaps he could be of some assistance, one of his oldest colleagues happened to be...If she would give him some particulars about herself he could write a note on her behalf. Why didn't she come by the hotel...? Bakti visualized her, the bony Marxist spreading herself on the shoddy hotel sheets, her soul kept pristine by the pretense that this was happening to her because she was a member of a certain class, trapped in certain circumstances. Historical inevitability! Bakti would like to present her with a few inevitabilities! Any Algerian girl would give ten years to be as free as the continually martyred Mlle. Arnaud.

He shook his head, trying to concentrate on the ledger. What were they arguing about? Borderline cases. Those one might be kind to for one reason or another and pass, or be strict with and fail. Let them jabber at it; Bakti had no wish to contribute. The expected viewpoints came forth; that one must not be too easy, the certificates must have genuine value, especially since the university was new, but that many students had been disadvantaged in language study because of the prohibition against almost all travel outside the country and the virtual absence of foreigners within it; that others were still more severely disadvantaged since they already were teachers at primary or secondary school level and could only come one day a week to class— almost half of the students were in this category. While the Oran certificates should be as difficult to obtain and as prestigious as those of the Sorbonne, Oxford, and Harvard, still, it must be understood that the students had been ill-favored and that we must certainly graduate some of them.

The Englishwoman now tried to help by telling an opaque anecdote about the Red Brick Universities when they had first opened. Mlle. Arnaud wanted to help too; she had witnessed the salutary effect on others of having failed examinations. They reprepared them so well. She could not speak from her own experience, but...Benslimane nodded eagerly. Up to this moment more than half the students had failed and would either waste months preparing for a retake of their examinations or would drop out of the university. Quite likely some of the girls who failed would be summarily married off by their impatient fathers. But Benslimane was apparently pleased that any kind of consensus could be reached.

Sledd now spoke up, his words in French struggled over separately, like the formations of a mechanical voice box. What he said, however, was sharply human. "If we failed this propor-tion of our students in America, we'd conclude that we hadn't taught them well enough."

"That is your point of view?" Carrere said, very coolly, apparently sincere.

And Sledd went right into it with statistics on intelligence and achievement which were virtually untranslatable from the American to any other culture, as Bakti knew. Then some philosophy, pertinent enough, about the necessity of training people for useful purposes, and the social disservice of keeping them overlong in schools. This, of course, was unpalatable to most of those in the room for whom staying power had been the principal ingredient of academic success.

In fact Carrere's coolness had already cued their attitudes so that when Carrere said, "Our point of view, on the other hand...," it was a genuine *our*, Bakti excepted. "Our point of view, on the other hand, is that it is the responsibility of the student to learn. We present the material; that is our responsibility. It is not our responsibility that the student succeed."

Sledd said, "Do you consider that you have no social responsibility?"

Crazy! An American, the lone "imperialist," for God knew how many bloody miles, talking social responsibility to a group of people everyone of whom would call himself a socialist! And here came the Cadet of the Revolution to gloss it all over.

"Perhaps," said the Cadet, "it is more responsible to discourage students sometimes, rather than give rise to false hopes."

"And, too," said Carrere, "there is the question of equivalence." After a brief silence. "There is no point in granting certificates and degrees which are not acceptable elsewhere."

The sweet reason of this statement, so casually and certainly pronounced, shot a jet of hysteria into Bakti's brain. What "elsewhere?" There was only one elsewhere so far as Carrere was concerned: the universities of France! Intellectual and cultural imperialism pure and simple! Trap Algerian students into a system which would lead them inevitably to France. No wonder Lyons had been happy to grant him leave to come here.

"Most students will not go elsewhere," Sledd said, apparently wishing honestly to enlighten Carrere. "Most will finish their education here and go directly into professional life. Shouldn't they be our first concern?"

Carrere said, "They most assuredly should be our first concern," subtly emphasizing the "our," "—most assuredly, and my concern is that they should be able to continue to higher studies."

Bakti said loudly, "In France, you mean."

After a second, Carrere said, "In France," and raised his shoulders. "French standards are accepted throughout the ...world."

Bakti knew that Carrere had almost said "*civilized* world." He said, "Perhaps *our* standards will be acceptable elsewhere too. In fact, to have what you call 'equivalence', our curriculum would have to be identical with that of a French university. We did not fight the Revolution for that."

A "Spaniard" said sharply, "Bakti!"

"And further I would say it would be unwise of us in the extreme to model our curriculum on one which has been considered in all quarters obsolete and socially valueless! The English section, at least, will not do so." The Englishwoman's cheeks were brilliant red; all eyes were downcast. "Now," Bakti said. "Let us go through the individual cases and be as just as we can. Mlle. Arnaud." He nodded to her. She cleared her voice and they started again around the circle.

Either opinions had been more polarized than Bakti had suspected or Sledd and Carrere had polarized them. The Carrere-side grades were all failing or barely passing while the Sledd-side's were all generous, some of them fatuously so. Clearly the grades were being changed as they were being read out! Naturally, Bakti thought, Carrere would want all but a tiny tame elite of Algerian students to fail! And of course Sledd would be easy! One had but to see him stooping down to a student for a consultation, helpfully taking the girls' elbows in his hand, always *agreeing* with them initially—miracles though that might require—until he spoke his own piece. More important, the American point of view would find a large Algerian elite of mediocre education desirable. Algeria should become a kind of new midwestern bread-and-oil basket to be manipulated by Washington and New York! Since there were no official diplomatic relations, who had allowed Sledd into the country?

Bakti slowed the proceedings to be certain that the grades were being shaded and became doubly convinced that they were. It did not take that long to read a figure from a column! He heard an absurdly low grade for Chiali, Ahmed, and hiked Chiali's grade in American Civilization two points when it came to his turn, scribbling a note to himself to rectify his ledger. The American gave Djezzar, Sidi Mohamed, a grade worthy of a genius and Bakti dropped him three points. So it went through the entire list.

When the final candidate, Tayeb, Fatiha, had been averaged and there had been no objections or amendments, Bakti said, "We have done our work." Carrere was smiling at him with wide, luminous eyes. Carrere had nothing but contempt for what he had seen, for what Bakti had done. Yet if *they* could play that game, why not Bakti? He was no longer the boy that every adult Frenchman had known was a thief and scoundrel, guilty of whatever they claimed he was. He should no longer know that breathless state in which it was impossible, treasonous to oneself, to attempt an explanation or make a case, or even shout if he wanted.

"We have finished," he said. "Let us break up."

He rose as did the others, all of them busily collecting their things as the chairs scraped. He delayed, wishing that they would get out the door ahead of him, but their haste and the arrogant tilt of Carrere's chin goaded, and he said, "Mlle. Arnaud, please." She waited clutching her notebooks to her bosom as the others filed out. She was sullen, her mouth fattening.

"Close the door," he said.

"No, I shall not."

"This university is not a French university."

Silence.

"We have no reason to accept French standards."

"What are your standards, then?"

"We will develop them." He was rubbing his scar with his thumb. "So long as you are on the faculty you would do well to remember it."

"That's what you wished to say to me?"

"The past is not entirely forgotten, Mlle. Arnaud."

"You like to be reminded of it, perhaps." This was sarcastic but in a different tone. She was very pale now.

"Everything today reminds me of it. Professor Carrere—"

"Oh, well," she interrupted. "You know he is very old school, conservative. You mustn't believe that every influence from France..." and so on, suddenly rather girlish, chattering away, worried about her job, he supposed. "...In any case that is over and done with now."

He said quietly, "I wish some things were over and done with."

Which silenced her. Her lips twitched and her fingers worked the edges of her notebooks. He could spread her out on *his* grubby sheets. Perhaps he would tie her ankles to the bed frame.

He said, "Our next meeting is tomorrow at nine. First year students."

"Yes." Pretending blindly to look at her watch.

"I will lock up."

She left. He heard her going quickly down the hall, heels not touching, chasing Carrere. He snapped his briefcase shut, closed the window, and locked the door behind him. The hall was partially flooded from the women's toilets. He picked his way out to the quadrangle where fires of uprooted weeds were smoldering between the lines of palms. The smoke plumes drifted upward, yellow in the sunlight, making the birds scold.

A girl appeared at his elbow. "Please, sir, can you tell me if I passed?" He could not for the moment think of her name, although she had been in his course. She smiled her plea, a thin, gray-skinned girl with mottled gums.

"No results available." His brusqueness rocked her backwards and clamped her mouth shut. Rather than softening him, the gesture annoyed him. "The grades are given to everyone at the same time."

"Yes, sir."

"There are no special cases."

"Yes, sir."

"You will have to wait." He nodded, dismissing her.

"Good-bye, sir." She turned awkwardly, stumbled off the single low step, then hurried away.

He could see Carrere and the others perhaps one hundred yards ahead of him, near the highway, neither strolling nor striding, walking clumsily together. He stepped down and scuffed his heel into the gravel roadway. He remembered the girl's name, Hassani, Rachida. I've done it to her, he thought.

He started walking, closing his mouth against the bitter smoke and squinting at the half-renovated buildings whose stucco walls were veined with white plaster repairs. The Faculte des Sciences on his left was an almost empty shell; there were chairs to sit on but little laboratory equipment. The Faculte de Medecine next it, which had been established longer, was better organized but less than half-staffed, and the General Hospital in the city was a chaos of overwork and incompetence.

There was everything to be done here, all new and to be accomplished.

Starting with himself.

ALPHONSE

I had "inherited" Alphonse from my predecessor in Texaco's Abidjan office and since there was no change in routine he went about his duties of cooking and keeping house with a minimum of questions. He was taciturn and a silent walker and mover of objects; he could barely be heard cleaning in the next room. And because of his quietness and because all ran smoothly I at first took him for granted and hardly noticed him. But day by day I became increasingly aware of his slight, stiffly erect figure passing barefoot from room to room, of his delicately made but roughened hands as he served at table, of his slow, almost sleepy "yes, seh" which was nonetheless comprehending. His gestures had a gravity which gave him presence, and his introspection had a curious force.

I would find him at the kitchen sink staring through the barred aperture above it at the underbrush which grew rank beyond the villa's plot, and would have to say his name to break his reverie. His face would turn, unstartled, and he would take a second or two to inquire, "Seh?" I was the taller by a head and shoulders and he would tilt back his head to speak, but there was nothing in the movement of cringing or of nervousness. His big, perhaps hyperthyroid eyes asked simply what was wanted. One day I asked him what he had been dreaming of and he answered in his slow voice that his sister in Daloa had borne a boy. After that I often questioned him. He was having a palaver with a meat seller in the market. Part of his roof had been blown away by a storm. They were ordinary things he told me and I sensed considerable reserve, but his absentmindedness created something like a third personality in the house, a welcome extension to my rather narrow life. And one of his habits charmed me.

The windows and doors of my villa were unscreened and at night when the lights were lit the ceilings and walls were dotted with insects and small, pink-transparent lizards which fed on them. These I did not mind but some of the other visitors I did— wasps, for instance, and roaches, and rhinoceros beetles which looked as big as chickens' eggs and had harder shells, stupid creatures who would fly straight into any obstruction (including myself), fall to the floor, recover themselves, and again smash into anything in their line of flight. The first time I called Alphonse to get rid of one I expected him to fetch a flyswatter or a broom and kill it. Not at all. He caught the beetle in the air, held it by its wings, and set it free outside. He handled wasps in the same way. Only roaches would he kill with a sharp smack of the bare ball of his foot, whether because a previous employer had insisted that he do so or because he had decided that that species would in any case survive, I do not know. Both his "reverence for life" and his physical feats in preserving it impressed me. He would look feeble and stiff following the bug's flight, then his hand would flick out, aimed perfectly, and he would have it unharmed. I once asked him his age. He told me he did not know, but he must have been forty at least.

One evening, perhaps a month after my arrival, I had several drinks at the club with a business acquaintance leaving on vacation and returned to my villa late for dinner. I was feeling irritated by a long day of work in the heat, by the dank atmosphere of the rainy season—the usual tropical complaints.

Sitting alone at the table I became annoyed with the weary shuffle of Alphonse's feet and his distracted staring while he waited, leaning against the sideboard, for me to finish eating. The coffee cup and saucer clattered in his hand when he brought them. As he was about to set them down the cup fell and smashed to the floor.

"You've been drinking," I said.

He remained silent and I looked up at him and repeated what I had said.

"Yes, seh," he said, surprising me.

"Why?"

He hesitated, staring at the dark window. "Have palaver, seh," he finally said.

"With whom?"

"Owner for house."

I expected him to go on to say that he had been unable to pay the rent and to ask for an advance in salary, but instead he drawled out that the owner was a Diula while he was of the Webe tribe. He shifted his feet. "Missus have no baby ones."

"What's that?"

"Diula man be bad man. He make bother for her." After a pause, "All Diula men be bad men."

I thought he was rambling. "This is the last time you'll be drunk working here," I said.

"Yes, seh."

He turned up next morning as quietly efficient as before, and remained so, and after a few days I had almost forgotten the incident. But two or three weeks later at lunch he was clearly slower than usual and his balance was uncertain. In answer to my questioning look he said, "I not well, seh."

"What's the matter?"

"I sick for head." He tapped his skull.

"Your head aches?"

"Yes, seh. Doctor say I sick for head."

"What doctor?"

"Doctor for Adjame." Adjame is the suburb of Abidjan in which Alphonse lived.

"Is he a European doctor?" I meant European-trained.

"No, seh. Doctor for Africans."

I got up from the table. "I'll give you some pills that will fix you up." He followed me to the bathroom, swallowed two aspirins, and took four more to the kitchen in case the headache persisted. Before leaving for the office I asked if he felt better.

"Yes, seh," he answered, but without conviction.

Although he continued to do his work conscientiously he was noticeably changed from that day on. His eyes were almost always dreamily veiled and I could tell from the movements of his lips that the dreams were dramatic. His retreat further heightened my awareness of him, but beyond offering more aspirin I did not know what to do.

Several nights later he was drunk again. I at first decided to ignore it. I was tired and did not want to get into a useless discussion or be forced to bawl him out. But after I had waited long minutes for the dessert and then found that he had forgotten it and was washing dishes, I asked, "Why are you drunk this time?"

His eyes came into focus, then he looked away. "Is Diula man, seh."

"What has he done?"

"Seh...he put fire in my bed."

"He burnt down your house?"

"No, seh, house all right."

"You got the fire out, then."

He hesitated, seeming almost to smile. "When I wake, big flames all around my bed."

"What did you do?"

"Doctor come, seh, make them go away."

"The *doctor*...?"

Every night I could hear drumming from some part of the city and I had grown so used to it that it no longer bothered my sleep. But that night I listened a long time. At breakfast I told Alphonse he must stop seeing this doctor and go instead to the government clinic to be treated by a European doctor. He looked dubious. "Will you go?"

"Cost too much money, seh."

"I'll give you the money. Look, I'll give you a thousand francs. You bring back the change." Since I had thrust the money into his hand he could hardly refuse it. That evening he returned half.

He said the doctor had given him some pills but although I did not accuse him, his uneasy manner made me suspect he had not been near the clinic.

His condition did not change. I gave him anything in the medicine chest which might possibly have some effect— vitamin pills, for instance. One evening the villa was shuttered tight when I got home from work.

Next morning I woke to the alarm clock, angry. I had slept badly and the sheets were soaked with sweat. I was brushing my teeth when I heard Alphonse's voice behind me, "Seh."

"Well, where the hell have you been?" I rinsed my mouth and turned around to say more but he looked so frail and sad, head down and shoulders slumped, that I kept silent.

"I too sick for work," he said.

"What's the matter now?"

"I tell you, seh, I sick for head."

"What's the trouble with your head? Does it ache?"

"No, seh. Doctor," he stopped, stared out the window a moment, and then at me. "Doctor take twenty-three bugs from head last night."

"Twenty-three *bugs*. What kind of bugs?"

"Be small and black, seh." He indicated the size with thumb and forefinger. "Doctor show them after."

"After what?"

"After I wake."

"Alphonse, this is impossible. He can't have taken any bugs from your head. Where do you think they came out?"

"From ear, seh. This night he get more. Have too many, he say."

"Listen to me, Alphonse." I was standing over him now, trying to convince him by the weight of my bigger voice and person. "It is not true that you have bugs in your head. Such a thing is impossible. Do you hear me?"

"Yes, seh."

"Believe me. I know."

He looked out the window and said, "He show me them."

"You go back to the European doctor and tell him what you've told me. He will tell you that I'm right."

"Yes, seh," he said, head down.

After I had dressed I went to the kitchen and met Joseph, whom Alphonse had brought as a replacement. He was already wearing Alphonse's uniform and cooking eggs. I gave Alphonse the salary I owed him and a tip, and assured him he could have his job back whenever he felt well enough to do it. He thanked me, shook hands, and walked slowly, somewhat unsteadily, out of the house.

Joseph was competent enough, good-natured, and quick-witted. I missed Alphonse and often asked for news of him. The reports never varied. "He is sick for his brain," Joseph would say with a broad, apologetic smile. But was he getting better? "Oh, yes. Soon be better."

One day at lunchtime I was pleased to see Alphonse walking in the drive; but my hopes that he had returned to work were quickly disappointed. He was thinner—his eyes seemed enormous—and his mouth sagged in a beaten line.

"How are you?"

"Get well, seh."

"You don't look well."

"Diula man take my strength."

"…What is it you want?"

"Need money, seh. Doctor, he ask more money."

"Which doctor."

"Doctor for clinic."

I did not believe him but he appeared to be so weak I felt I could neither argue nor refuse. I gave him a thousand francs, returned depressed to my lunch, and told Joseph how Alphonse had been.

"Yes, I hear him too."

"What's the matter with him?" I asked, not really expecting an answer, just wanting to talk. "Do you know?"

"Alphonse cheat you," he said, turning away.

"Cheated me?"

"In market, seh. He buy something, pay one price and tell you another, and with the money remaining…" Joseph lifted an imaginary bottle and drank.

"You mean liquor is his sickness?"

Joseph nodded. "Drink too much wine every day. At night he sick for brain. When Alphonse come again, master should not give him money."

"Thank you," I said. "I won't."

So I thought, finally, that I understood. Alphonse was having attacks of *delerium tremens* and the native doctor's ignorance was compounding the trouble. Lacking a diagnosis, he had invented the "bugs" in Alphonse's head to preserve his reputation, and Alphonse was failing largely because he had been convinced that he was mentally rotten, seriously diseased.

I brooded about him that night and for many nights afterwards. To what extent was I responsible for his condition? I had been careless, yes, but could the victim of thievery be held responsible for the thief? If I had sometimes gone with him to the market and checked the prices so that he would not have dared to cheat me would he, anyhow, have found the money to drink himself into this condition?

There were, of course, no certain answers, only further, deeper questions. Just recently the French administration had lowered the price of North African wine (which was transported to the Ivory Coast in tank ships, like fuel) so that an African could get drunk more cheaply on wine than on English gin—traditionally the Africans' favorite liquor. And this official action logically derived from the colonial policy of grafting European needs and vices onto the African population in order to sell more goods. I was American and sold petroleum products and so did not directly profit from the sale of wine, but I was nonetheless a member of the European community and the fortunes of my company, and thus my own, rose and fell, broadly speaking, with the community's. If I benefitted from Alphonse's drinking, no matter how remotely and slightly, was I then responsible for his cure? Like most people's, the assumptions of my education were that everyone has a right to make his own decisions, to think what he pleases, and so on. But if you have in front of you a man with an infected cut who refuses through fear or ignorance to put some disinfectant on it when the stuff is available to him, what do you do then? The cut may become gangrenous; the man may lose a limb, or his life. If you command him to stand still, and he obeys, you apply the iodine and remove—as far as you can—those possibilities. If you accept his refusal and the man continues to suffer you must also accept that there was something you might have done to prevent it. You have sacrificed his health to a principle, perhaps to vanity in your principles. But any denial of his right to refuse seems in your eyes to degrade both him and you, he because he is expected to comply like a slave or child, and you because you are treating him as a piece of machinery you do not want out of order or, at best, as an extension of your own self: you would force yourself to apply iodine to a cut of your own, thus you will force it on him. In either case you are treating him as something less than a free man and no matter what his degree of ignorance and superstition you must want to give him that much dignity.

I remained undecided for some time. I believed there was a chance of convincing Alphonse that wine was his sickness. Still, he had the African doctor. ...Finally I resolved at least to see him and asked Joseph to tell him so: that I wanted to visit him, or, if he preferred and felt strong enough, that he should come to the villa. But Alphonse had left Adjame. Joseph discovered he had been taken to a village some forty miles inland where relatives of his could care for him. That had encouraged me; I assumed the doctor had remained in Adjame. The next Sunday after breakfast Joseph and I got in my car and went to find him.

We drove through Adjame's busy marketplace and soon were in the rain forest, the tires singing on the newly laid asphalt. The villages we passed had been ripped open by bulldozers widening the road bed, and the exposed jumbles of huts made me try to imagine with increasing uncertainty our reception at our destination. It seemed to me I had forgotten the primitiveness of the hinterland.

I stopped and Joseph asked the way. Then we continued another ten miles. The turnoff was unmarked but plainly visible, for a bearded goatherd was driving his flock out of it and across the highway. The side road was a tunnel through high, thick forest, potholed and rough. Joseph held the door handle in order not to be thrown across the seat. When the sun shone, chinks of yellow filtered through the foliage; when clouds obscured it the light turned a strange green dusk in which Joseph's skin, a chocolate brown, looked greasily black. We came to a village—a semicircle of huts that had pushed the forest back thirty or forty feet from the road—and while Joseph talked the children gathered, the boys naked and the girls wearing bead belts which held strips of red cloth between their legs, to stare at my Chevrolet and me.

The road forked and became still rougher and narrower.

"Near here, seh."

I could see nothing but forest, not a hut, a person, or a path.

"Stop here," Joseph said. "Must walk from here."

As I turned off the ignition the whirrs and buzzes of insects and the songs and notes of birds bore in. The noise was possessive, like the roar of a waterfall. Hundreds of small white butterflies fluttered around my legs when I stood in the road.

"Come."

The path was clear enough once we were on it, a track of beaten earth winding through underbrush so thick I had to look straight up to see the taller trees. Flies zinged past my ears and one drew blood biting my leg. No breeze could penetrate here and the humid air felt soft.

Cocoa trees appeared, planted near the path, and I faintly heard a pestle thumping meal. When we turned the final corner perhaps a dozen people were staring at us from the middle of the village compound, a barren area ringed irregularly by poor huts. When we stopped at the compound's edge, what must have been the entire population, Alphonse excepted, had come out to look us over. Joseph spoke, and a gray-headed man dressed in a kente cloth toga and leaning on a staff came toward us and nodded to me in a friendly way. While Joseph talked to him I looked around, at the withered dugs of an old woman squatting by a low fire, at a little girl's protruding belly button (almost all the children had navel hernias), at a homemade flintlock rifle leaning against a wall. I became self-conscious and impatient with Joseph's conversation, but I did not interrupt. Finally, he introduced me to the elder, and said, "He say Alphonse too sick. Some days past he chase people with machete."

"Chase people?"

"Try to kill them." The elder nodded vigorously.

"Where is he now?"

Joseph pointed to a conical, thatch-roofed hut at the far end of the compound. "They hold him there."

"Let's go see him."

"Wait, seh." A stocky mulatto, Europeanized by shorts, undershirt, and a pair of plastic sandals was joining us. "This be doctor."

"The Adjame doctor?"

Joseph nodded.

The doctor's mouth was wide and hooked down at the ends in an expression of grave medical confidence. Not a trace of welcome, interest, humor, suspicion—of anything—touched his face as he shook my hand. The man who took bugs from Alphonse's ears.

Joseph exchanged a few words with him. "Can see Alphonse now."

The village was silent while the three of us crossed to the hut. I stooped to pass through the door and at first could see only that Alphonse was lying on the ground. As my eyes adjusted to the light I saw that his back was to me and that a loincloth was his only clothing. I squatted and said his name and he struggled to roll over, and I then saw that what I had taken to be a stool at his feet was in fact a primitive stocks. His right leg disappeared at midcalf into a hollowed section of log and his foot was trapped at its other end by a system of chocks held in place by strips of leather. Looking at it, I became aware of the hut's smell, a gagging mixture of sweat and excrement.

Alphonse propped himself on his elbows and stared at me. He was very thin and his windpipe and tendons stood out in his neck.

"Hello, Alphonse."

"Hello, seh." His voice cracked on the polite tones. He knew who I was, I supposed, but there was no recognition in his dulled eyes.

"How are you?"

"All right, seh."

"You have grown thinner. Do you get enough to eat?"

An automatic, "Yes, seh."

Joseph said, "They give him food but he not eat it."

Alphonse muttered something that I could not understand.

"You don't look well," I said, and he stared at me in silence.

Then Joseph spoke in dialect and after a time Alphonse made some sort of reply, punctuating it by rolling back his head to look at the doctor who was standing quietly against the wall. Joseph said, "He too sick, seh."

"Ask the doctor how long he's been lying here, and how much longer he expects he will be."

The answer was, "Some days," and a shrug of the shoulders.

I leaned down to Alphonse and said slowly, "You are not well here, Alphonse. I think you should come back to Adjame."

"Adjame," he repeated, as though the name produced distant memories.

"I will take you back. Come with Joseph and me in the car."

"Car?"

"Yes, we came in the car."

"Am well here, seh."

"Alphonse, listen to me. Wine, not bugs, has made you sick. I will put you in a hospital. You will get good care..." The word "hospital" had brightened his eyes and I stopped momentarily. "Yes, hospital, Alphonse."

He shook his head. "No, seh. Stay here. Stay here, seh." He dropped from his elbows to the ground and when I leaned forward to see his face he drew his fists to his chin, cringing. "No, seh. No," he croaked, thrashing his head back and forth.

Joseph gripped my arm. "No use to talk. We go now."

Alphonse was babbling, "Hospital, no. No, seh." Joseph pulled my arm with authority and I looked at him amazed. No African had ever bossed me.

"Come," he said, and stood up, still holding my arm. I followed him out and stopped, dizzy, the glare hurting my eyes. "Do no good," he said.

I looked from him to the doctor who stood on my other side. His mouth wore the same expression of diagnostic certainty. Following Joseph's lead I shook his hand and he nodded gravely, as though I had confirmed his opinion. "Let's go," I said to Joseph.

The elder stopped us at the entrance to the compound. Joseph translated, "He think master find this a good village."

"A fine village," I said. "Tell him 'very fine.'"

Walking on, a woman's voice called Joseph's name. I went ahead to the car and when he joined me I asked what she had wanted.

"She say Alphonse soon go far away."

"And who is she?"

"That woman? Be wife to Alphonse."

I drove back to the villa in silence, went inside, and poured myself a drink.

I did not dare ask for several weeks and when I had found that courage I did not dare for a moment to look at Joseph's face. I heard his feet shuffle. "Alphonse go far away," he said, waving his hand in the air. "Too far away." And I knew that he had died. Joseph was smiling slightly, head cocked to one side, and I thought, or imagined, that I recognized sympathy and something else—a look of strength which told me what was and what was not my business. Later, I remembered how Alphonse had caught the wasps and rhinoceros beetles and set them free outside, and wondered how I might have done as well by him.

WHELPS OF WAR

We had been mustered over the PA system, eight of us for a work party, and we waited together on the fantail until the chunky Greek coxswain, Krikorian, shouted attention and told us we were to take one of the landing boats in to General Stores, Manila, load it with rations, and provision every captured Japanese ship in the bay!

"Admiral" Nelson, a gunner's mate from Georgia said, "You mean we're gonna sweat our ass for *them?*"

"You read me, 'Admiral,'" Krikorian said. "Prisoners of war, they got a right to eat. Geneva 'ventions." Krikorian was bucking to go regular Navy and you could see that in the way he about-faced and saluted the gangway officer and then checked us off on a clipboard as we went over the side.

There was silence in the boat. Nelson was up forward by himself and others sat on the engine housing amidships with their backs to one another. I leaned on the outboard combing, looking at the bows and bridges of the sunken ships which jutted at strange angles out of the shallow water. All of them had been freighters, some ours sunk by the Japanese taking the Philippines, some Japanese sunk by us returning. Rust had flaked the ships' names off the hulls so that they could have been either nationality. At night, alone on the bridge on signal watch, I made up stories about them, working out itineraries and involvements in battles from the history of the war, in which neither I nor our ship, the USS Walter B. Cobb, APD 106, had fired or heard a shot after training. I had scarcely heard one at all, since I had enlisted at seventeen and had come aboard as a replacement only two months before in San Diego, a week before the Japanese surrendered.

General Stores was up a canal in downtown Manila which was a dusty, smelly mess of broken streets and walls in which thousands of slender brown people were constantly moving, tote-yokes over their shoulders, trading, putting together makeshift places to live in the bombed out shells. We passed the liberty landing and were called to by the busiest people of all—the crowd of ragtag pimps around the gate.

Nelson yelled at them, "Fuck y'own sisters, fuckin' gooks."

"You think they do that, Admiral?"

He was furious. "Fuckin' gook do any fuckin' thing."

We tied up and filed into the warehouse behind swaggering Krikorian. There were handcarts and dollies for our use, and they saved labor, but the heat inside was cruel. We panted, loading, and rushed out to the boat, dogging it in the outside air for as long as we could. When we had the consignment aboard, Krikorian gave us a break and we flopped down on the dock. He was worrying over the location of the Japanese ships and whether anyone aboard them could speak English.

"I'd as leave deep six the stuff," a deckhand said.

"I got my orders," Krikorian said, turning on him. "Orders is orders." He got the chart out of the boat and went to find someone who'd confirm the ships lay where he thought they did.

"He can stuff it."

When Krikorian came back he said, "OK, men, got the course laid out now. Let's get to her. Inna boat now." As we clambered aboard over the cases and sacks he said, "All right, assholes, move it. You think I'm liking this any better than you?"

Which made me realize that a part of me was liking it—I was curious about the Japanese. On our voyage out we'd put in at Guam and had been given an afternoon's liberty in a navy beer garden. The area was kept clean by a detail of Japanese prisoners guarded by SPs with shotguns, and watching them I'd found it hard to believe such men could have attacked us. They were so small, frail-looking, it seemed their hands could hardly get around the broom handles. Often when a sailor had finished a can of beer he would throw it at one of them and if it hit, on the head or anywhere, the Japanese would pick it up without a trace of anger, without a glance, and put it in one of the garbage cans. How had they managed to hurt us?

When we had cleared the canal I scrambled over some crates— condensed milk, for example, what would they do with condensed milk?—to the wheel. Krikorian was happy to show me the chart. "Figure this'n be that DE, or like our DE, there." Her bow and stack were a bit more sharply swept than our destroyer escorts; her color was a little lighter. She flew no flags—an astonishing thing for a ship, bare as something newborn—but, closer, there was nothing fresh about her. She needed paint, needed to be chipped and sanded, zinc oxidized, and then painted, and before a crewman's face was distinct you could see their uniforms were in tatters. All kinds of clothes they had—T-shirts of odd sizes, trousers and chopped off trousers, caps and hats, and the damndest variety of shoes! Basketball shoes with rubber disks on the ankles, brown work boots up to midcalf, black slippers, and some of them were barefoot. Coming alongside, several in our crew spat over the side, and the Japanese, whose feet were at about eye level, did the same, not at, but towards us. Krikorian idled the engine and yelled, "Spikka de English?"

An officer—gold bars on a shirt half bleached out, like camouflage cloth—stepped to the head of their ladder and said, oddly, "English here."

"Bloody limey," someone said.

"Gotta provisions," Krikorian shouted, making spooning motions.

"Very well," said the officer. "Please to throw lines." He singsonged some orders and several Japanese stepped to the rail but none of us picked up the lines until Krikorian barked. I threw the bowline and it hit a man in the ribs and he and his partner yammered at me. Both were squat, big knots in their legs and thick necks, and their jaws seemed to work in an odd way, not really closing on their words. How would they have liked the line thrown? Goddamnit, there was only one way to throw a line!

I shouted, "Shut your stupid mouths!" and they all began to chatter, maybe twenty men milling around, not threatening us exactly, but still, there were more of them than us and they were above us. Krikorian drew his sidearm automatic and now he waved it over his head. They mainly stopped moving and their voices dropped.

We got braced against the DE's ladder and the two crews formed irregular chains to pass the cases along. "OK," said Krikorian, and handed me the list of provisions. I read it off: dehydrated potatoes, powdered scrambled eggs, a case of baked beans. They weren't turning anything down. Their man at the head of the ladder was plucking the cases out of our man's hands so quickly he was always ready for the next one. Someone said, "Hurry it up, mates, we're falling behind."

At the end of the list I said, "That's all for these birds, Krik."

"Finish!" he yelled at the officer. "Cast off the lines!" They were confused, perhaps they thought the entire boatload was for them, and they didn't move to the cleats. "Lines!" Krikorian yelled. "Lines!" Still they didn't move and I had an instant nightmare: they were going to fall on us. I jumped to the bowline wanting to cast it off from our side, and then they understood. A couple of them smiled, perhaps at my fear, chucking the lines down into the boat.

We headed for a second DE in about the same condition as the first. And the same routine: confusion, Krikorian waving his automatic around, the lines going over the side. This crew was comparatively well dressed, lots of tan baseball caps with insignia on the brow. I started reading off the same menu, "Four cases dehydrated spuds," and heard a thump and a noise that was something like a shriek. The Japanese were all looking at the end man in our chain—Nelson, he'd moved. He was taking a second case from the man behind him and when he had it at shoulder height he launched it like a shotput at the nearest Japanese legs—and hit them. The man crumpled forward, mouth open, eyeglasses flying off, then fell backward to the deck, and scuttled away on hands and knees.

"Ho!" went Krikorian.

"Yeah, Admiral!"

Others laughed, including me. He threw the third case from his waist, more like the hammer throw, and it sailed higher than the shotput, but it hit nothing, landing on, and collapsing, one of its corners.

The Japanese had scattered back from the ladder. "Gimme somethin' lighter," Nelson said to me.

"Two powdered eggs."

When he had them he yelled at the Japanese, "Misuble chickens!" They didn't move and his two throws were harmless, landing beyond the potatoes.

There was some Japanese talk and a man darted in to drag away a case of eggs. Nelson picked up a third case of eggs and waited, but they were watching him. Krikorian said, "They're on to you, Admiral. Hold up till the next ship." Nelson threw what remained as hard as he could anyway, and a case of condensed milk broke open and the cans ran around, the Japs chasing them.

They threw down our lines—Krikorian was waving his automatic again—and we pulled away. Krikorian said to me, "Tell the Admiral just two PCs left. Ought to have lower decks."

I took the message to him but he was very red, drenched with sweat, and didn't pay much attention. The PC's deck was certainly lower, and apparently they had seen us at the DEs for they were ready to tie us up. They did that sloppily enough, discipline appeared to be lax, but they wouldn't come near the gangway to take the cases from Nelson. He waited, but they wouldn't budge from an arc outside his range. He said, "Don't give 'em the rations, Krik. I'll bust your ass, you do."

"You want go on report, Admiral?" To me, Krikorian said, "Read the list."

I did and others shoved the provisions aboard while Nelson swore. The Japanese watched him, shuffling their feet and crossing their arms.

The final PC was anchored quite separately from the other three ships. The man on watch looked stupefied as we approached. "Ain't seen us," Nelson said. "Ain't, by God, seen us."

Krikorian's shout made the watchman jump through a hatch, and some seconds later he came back with an officer. Krikorian went through his pantomime again, and as he spooned, more Japanese came out on the fantail. These were in the poorest condition of all, a lot of them with ulcerated skins and patchy heads of hair.

I said, "Everything that's left's for them, Admiral."

"Put it all right here," he said, pointing at the engine housing. "Gonna get it off like automatic fire."

We stacked the cases, Nelson spitting on his hands, and, yes, the Japanese were making a chain from the gangway to a cargo hatch and there was a man with a shaved head, wearing bib overalls, at the head of the ladder waiting for Nelson to hand him something. Nelson hefted a case of beans, the heaviest kind of case, up to his shoulder and jounced it there, securing his grip. Overalls didn't move. Nelson's back foot was braced, his arm came back and he shot the case forward—*missed*! He had slipped and was draped over the combing, his head in the boat's well, and the case had gone off to the right of the Japanese and was bumping harmlessly over their deck.

Nelson came up cursing and there was no question the Japanese had understood his intention for they quickly got back from the ladder, pointing and jabbering.

Nelson tapped the next biggest man in our crew, and they climbed up on the engine housing and picked up a case between them. One, two, three! It sailed maybe fifteen feet in the air and came down in the middle of their fantail and broke apart, cans of beans rolling everywhere. One, two, three! And cans of milk were added. Then the powdered eggs, at least one sack of which punctured, for there was a spray of egg yellow, and the potatoes, until everything had been delivered and lay in a crazy heap.

"Lines!" Krikorian yelled, "Lines!"

I shook the bowline and a couple of them came gingerly to the side and cast us off, and once the lines were in the boat and there was a little water between us and the PC there was a strange sound, Japanese laughter. They were looking at us and at the pile of stuff and laughing! Nelson leaped up on the gunwhale to jump for their ladder but two men, then more, grabbed him and wrestled him back to the deck. Krikorian gunned the engine and we pulled away and the further we got, the louder, somehow, was the Japanese laughter.

Nelson stopped fighting and they let him up. The back of his head had been cut and blood was running down and around his neck.

"I didn't hit but one of them," he said. "I didn't hit but one."

He shook his head, saying it over and over again, and then began to sob. "Couldn't hit...but one of them!" His great shoulders heaved as he leaned on the forward combing. "Just...a goddamn one of 'em!"

Krikorian tapped me to take the wheel, went to Nelson, and patted his back.

"Just only a goddamn one of 'em!" Nelson said furiously and let out a bellow of a sob.

"You done real good, Admiral," Krikorian said. "Real good. Ain't anyone coulda done better."

Nelson shook Krikorian's hand away and wiped his cheekbones.

Krikorian said again. "You done good, Admiral."

Nelson's knuckles were white as he gripped the combing. "Couldn't even...break me a leg," he said. "Not even."

Krikorian began, "Ain't anyone—" Nelson turned and decked him, hit him one hard punch with his right hand and Krikorian was flat on his back, blinking, trying to raise his head. A couple of men jumped to him. Nelson thought they were coming to retaliate and dropped into a crouch. So did they. Krikorian sat up and spat out part of a tooth, a gleaming white dot on the bilge boards. The two men helped him to his feet. He made a gargling sound, spat over the side and said hoarsely, "You're on report, Admiral."

"If'n you do that..."

Someone shouted, and I turned to see we were about to ram a U.S. destroyer under its bows. I yanked the wheel over and the boat careened, and I could hear the others grabbing for holds and falling, lots of cursing.

We cleared the destroyer and I was lost for a minute. The gray water and sky had no dividing line, and the Cobb, when I located her, seemed to be floating in the air, and the bridge to be floating above the hull.

Krikorian yelled at me, "On course! On course!"

"Take the wheel yourself," I said, and left it.

The back of Nelson's hand had been jaggedly ripped from the first knuckle to his wrist. He was squeezing his hand white with his left hand, lots of blood running down his forearm. "Fucking sharp Greek teeth," Nelson said.

I looked at Krikorian at the wheel, and the men who had gathered near him, "regular" types, guys who sucked up to him. Krikorian said something to them, nodded his head at Nelson and the rest of us, and spat over the side.

At last, we had our war.

MARKLE AND
THE MOUSE

M arkle followed Ernie down the ladder to the liberty launch and they elbowed through their crowded shipmates to the starboard combing. They faced outboard, staring across Subic Bay at the navy yard's white buildings which wriggled in the heat and at the thickly jungled hills beyond. At an order, the cast-off lines thumped on the floorboards behind them; the launch reared back as the motor roared.

Markle said quietly, "Easiest thing you ever did, wasn't it?"

"Just about," Ernie said. "I was nervous, but now I wouldn't care if they hung me when we get back."

"I knew they wouldn't check the liberty list," said Markle. "They never do... and I got Gourley's beer chits, so everything's smooth."

The vibration of the launch seemed the only movement on the calm of the water. As they neared shore the tall palm trunks stood out of the shade and the beach was powder white under the sun. Two boats from other ships were already tied at the landing.

"Hey, Ernie."

Markle turned to see big Shafe, the coxswain, tapping Ernie's shoulder. Two men from the deck force stood beside him. "Ernie," Shafe said. "Ain't you kinda young to be drinking beer?"

"I don't think so," Ernie said.

"It seemed to me your Daddy and your Ma mightn't like it if they knew you was drinking beer."

"They don't mind, Shafe."

"What do *you* want?" Markle spoke loudly over the motor's noise, but Shafe did not answer. He stuck his hands in his hip pockets and his gold earring swayed and glittered. He continued, "I'm not certain you oughta be on this boat, Ernie."

Markle interrupted him again. "That's none of your business, Shafe."

"Mark," said Shafe, turning quickly, "you're gettin' *big* since you're first class flags, now ain't you? Pretty big since they give you three stripes and this kid to boss. Recollect, Mark: I can talk pretty loud sometimes."

"It wouldn't be worth your while," said Markle. "I can put you on report anytime I want."

Shafe moved slowly from heel to toe, first his gut then his face close to Markle. "You report me and I'd advise you not to walk alone too often. That's the way I'd advise you."

"I'd advise you not to get grabby with the kid's beer chits, Shafe. Lay off him."

Shafe spat over the combing. "I believe maybe right now you and the kid are alone too often. I wouldn't stay up late, neither."

Markle cursed him. Ernie had not moved. His face was solemn as the two deckhands leaned close to Shafe and the three talked. Then Shafe shrugged and moved off. "Don't let that deck monkey scare you," Markle said. "There's a lot around like him. He's phony, he's scareder than you are."

At the pier the men scrambled over the side and hurried toward the recreation area. Back from the beach, beneath the trees, were tables and benches on a concrete floor, and in the nearest Quonset was a window where the men drew their beer ration— six cans each. Ernie and Markle got their twelve—Ernie's on

Gourley's chits—and they carried him toward the tables. Small crowds had collected, and Markle and Ernie stopped at the first table where Shafe was standing next to a sailor with four pairs of dice in front of him. "What do you cut?" Shafe was asking.

"One out of six," the sailor said. "Nothing on side bets."

Shafe whistled and Markle shook his head.

"Do better," the sailor said. "Look around."

As he and Ernie walked away, Markle said, "Maybe a few side bets later on, but one out of six! Jesus!"

At the end of the next table they found room and sat down. They opened their first beers and in big successive gulps drank half before they put them down. Down the area a basketball game had started in an open court. A few had stripped off their clothes and were swimming; and far out beyond them the DE 101 lay slim and pretty, spotless in the distance.

They drank their second round, pouring the beer into paper cups stacked on the table. The thirds they treated as casually as their cigarettes.

His third cup empty, Markle left the table. Beyond the concrete, four urinals, vertical pipes with funnels slanted from their tops, were arranged in a cluster like loudspeakers. Standing there, his sight strayed through the trees to the open fields, and beyond them to the Philippine village which had been off-limits since the peace.

Then, at the base of a tree some ten yards away, he noticed a mouse nestled among the roots. He buttoned up and moved slowly towards the mouse, stalking it, cupped his hands, and bent at the knees. In one quick fall of the hands the mouse was caught.

"What you got there, Mark?"

"Where'd you find him?"

Markle went to the table. The mouse wriggled and tried to scratch until Ernie took it and stroked its head, gently tracing the delicate ears.

"I always did like mice," Ernie said. "I used to have a couple of white ones."

"Cute little bugger," Markle said. "Used to like them myself. I wonder is it true they can give you disease."

"Yeah," said another man. "I wouldn't fool with him like that."

"Lemme see him," said Shafe's voice.

"What do you want with him?" Markle asked.

"I ain't gonna hurt him."

"You won't hold him right," Ernie said.

"What way do you think I'll hold him—in my teeth?"

Ernie took one of the paper cups from the stack and gently put the mouse in it. "This way you can all have a look," he said, and gave the cup to Shafe.

Shafe looked a moment, then passed the cup on. Some put their fingers in to see if the mouse would nibble, and some tried to stroke its head. Even the dice games lost customers to the hunched and bright-eyed animal. When the cup had gone full circle, Shafe took it again and held it close to his chest, peering down at it. "I got a idea," he said. "I got a helluva idea."

"What *kind* of idea?" Markle said.

Shafe started away from the table toward the far end of the concrete.

"What *kind* of idea?" Ernie shouted. He and Markle jumped up and followed, pushing ahead through the others. At the edge of the floor, Shafe stopped and held up his hand.

"Men," he yelled, "you come on with me and we'll have us the best and biggest gamblin' game ever's been in Subic. Can you load a mouse? I ask, can you load a mouse? And I ain't cuttin' one for six, neither. Now come on, we'll find us a place to have it."

"Give me that mouse," said Ernie. "Give me that damned mouse."

Shafe held the cup above his head with one arm and Ernie from him with the other. "Now lookit here," he said to Ernie, "I ain't gonna hurt your damn mouse, you come along and see. And I'll give him back to you, once the game's done."

"Give it me, Shafe."

"Ah, hell," said Markle, "let him keep it. If it looks like he'll hurt him, we'll take him back."

Shafe already was walking down the area, the crowd close after him. They passed the basketball court and the swimmers before Shafe found a piece of flat ground he said was big enough. It lay back from the beach between the scattered palms. Shafe took a marlinspike from his belt and drew a small circle in the loose ground. Then, cursing the crowd to give room, he drew lines outward from the little circle, pie-cut lines, eight of them, all around the compass, and drew a big circle at their ends. "Choose your cut!" he yelled. "And lay your bets. Which way does he go? Which way's the mouse gonna run?"

The men spread out around the circle, digging for money in their pockets.

Markle stood at the edge of the big circle, Ernie just behind him.

Shafe yelled, "You get the odds of the board, seven to one on what you bet. Winner pays me deucer. OK? Well, lay 'em down boys, lay 'em right on down."

Markle laid two dollars and there were three other bets in the same cut. He said to Ernie, "Why don't you play the next cut and we'll split, win or lose."

"I'm not going to bet."

"Why not? Not bad odds."

"No, I won't bet."

When the bets were laid, Shafe moved them back from the line. "Shut your mouths," he said, "or this mouse won't never get out. You ready?" And he shook the cup, turned it upside down in the little circle, and walked away.

The mouse was motionless a moment and then began to scurry, away from the center but in various directions. Voices all around the circle urged it to them. Behind the sweat-drenched men, Shafe dodged, following the mouse's direction. The mouse came within an inch of winning for the cut directly opposite Markle's, then ran to the right, then finally crossed the line. Shafe pushed through the crowed, jammed the cup down, and poked the mouse into it from below. He set the cup in the center of the circle and collected and paid off the bets. Only a dollar and a half had been laid on the winning cut. Shafe must have made twenty.

He said, "An' this mouse gonna run some more. You can see my mouse ain't loaded, cain't you? Well, choose your cut and lay your money!"

No one left the circle and more were coming to it from the beer garden. The men were two or three deep all around.

Markle bet another two dollars. "Come on and bet," he said to Ernie.

"He's going to hurt that mouse."

"Ah, *hell*," said Markle, "he's all right."

Shafe shook the cup for the second game and upended it with a flourish. The mouse's coat was scuffled and sandy and when he moved he was less quick on his paws. He scurried, then sat a while, scurried, paused, and finally ruffled the line near the point of his first crossing. But this time he had crossed so close to a pie-line it was doubtful who had won. The men rushed forward to look at the tracks before Shafe had cupped the mouse, and for a minute the animal was lost among the feet.

"Christ! Did I hurt him?"

"Naw," said Shafe, "it's a real tough bugger, this mouse." He named the winners, collected, paid, and spieled for the third game.

Markle said, "It looks like they got a mouse magnet over there," but put down another two dollars.

Shafe was shaking the cup and the crowd was calling at the mouse.

"Which way does he run?" yelled Shafe. And they sang back, "Right to Poppa," and, "That mouse'll know a good man."

Shafe emptied the cup. The mouse was on its side, then wiggled upright and sat still, facing Markle. Its tufted coat was wet in patches. It sat still so long that Shafe walked out and looked at him. "He's OK," Shafe said. "Get hoppin', mouse." Shafe dropped a pebble near him, the mouse moved, and the crowd said, "Ah," but he had not scurried, he had pushed himself along the ground, unnaturally, as though one paw were stiff.

"Listen, Mark, that mouse—"

"Shut up. Come on, mouse, home to Poppa. Keep on pushing, mousey, push for Poppa." Markle went to one knee talking to it.

Ernie stood beside Markle, his eyes on the mouse who pushed towards Markle's cut, coming to them, rolling on its side after each motion, then righting itself to push again. Close to the edge it stopped, twitched its nose, and was still. Blood was on its hindquarters and its right hind paw stuck out from its side like a half-torn match.

Ernie pushed past Markle into the circle and stepped hard on the mouse.

"You son of a bitch!" Markle shouted beside him. "You son of a bitch, we'd-a-won! We'd-a-won, you dumb bastard!"

More of the men jumped forward, but stopped, knowing the mouse was dead. There was a mumble, then a jump in the noise when Shafe got through the crowd, and then quiet when Shafe stood facing Ernie. Ernie lifted his foot and shook off the wet, almost flattened body. Rivulets of sweat rolled down Shafe's red face and his earring jiggled.

"Get him, Shafe," the crowd talked. "Fix that little bastard good."

Shafe said over his shoulder, "Hold Mark." Markle struggled but they soon had him on the ground with his arms pinned behind him.

Ernie watched them, motionless.

"You ready, kid?" asked Shafe, cocking his fists. "You all set to go?"

"Knock it out of him, Shafe. Knock his ears off. Fix that little bastard, *good*."

"You better put 'em up, kid. I ain't-a-gonna dance."

Ernie said nothing. His arms hung loosely. Shafe hit him lightly on the chest and Ernie's arms came up as he clumsily stepped backwards. The crowd was noiseless. Shafe little-stepped, wide-legged, forward. Ernie threw out his left hand; Shafe swung and Ernie again went backwards on his heels. When he had his balance, he jogged to the right.

"You ain't runnin' away, kid? You ain't got a mind to run away?"

"He ain't gettin' through here, Shafe."

Ernie came into range and was hit on the stomach. Then he clicked Shafe's jaw with a wild right arm swing, and Shafe's face splotched purple. Now Shafe moved more quickly. He cuffed Ernie upright with a left, and hit him hard on the cheek. Ernie fell backward and rolled, and then came half up on his knees, his face against his forearm. His back swayed but he made no sound, no motion to rise.

Shafe walked toward him. Someone in the crowd said, "Say, that's good enough, Shafe," but the others were silent. He gripped Ernie under the arms and pulled him to his feet. Then he pushed Ernie from him with his left hand, said, "Heh!" so Ernie would lift his head, and hit him with the right. Ernie took two falling backward steps and landed loose and empty in the center of the circle. His feet splayed duckfoot, and his right arm lay askew across his chest. Blood ran from his nose and made a texture with the dirt already there.

Shafe walked to him and around him with his hands still fisted. He stopped, and looked at the quiet, uneasy men. He said, "Let go of Mark."

They released Markle and he took time getting up, shaking and rubbing his limbs. Then he stood on the line of the circle and looked at Shafe, unmarked but as open faced as Ernie.

"Mark," said Shafe, "come on a pace."

Markle stepped toward him hang-limbed; his face was blank.

Shafe said, "I ain't gonna hurt you, Mark. I ain't-a-even gonna *touch* you."

Markle's head nodded.

"What I want from you, Mark, is you go back, take out your money, and lay it in the cut. You do that, Mark."

"Yah," Markle said, "yah." His hands fluttered towards his pockets as he backed away.

"Give him room," Shafe growled at the crowed, then, "Lay 'em down, boys, lay out all you got. Last game today. The final and deciding." He walked around Ernie. "Lay down your money and stand back from the circle." He squatted near Ernie in the center. "Which way does he go, boys?" Shafe said. "Which way will he crawl?" He was watching the crowd. "Which way does he go, boys, which way will he crawl," as they laid their bets. Kneeling by his money was Markle, knowing it was lost.

Then Ernie moved and Shafe stepped away from him out of the circle.

ALL RIGHT

My mother's stance as she told us, summoned and seated, that our father would "have us" for the summer and that this would be an annual arrangement did not encourage questions. In a week my mother's cook and a maid would go with us children by overnight train to North Haven, Maine, where he had rented a house. We had never seen North Haven but neither Sage, who was thirteen, nor, I, eleven, nor Jill, seven, expressed much curiosity.

He met us in the city at the Grand Central Station gate. He looked business-brown in the yellowish light except for a new straw hat with a bright, polka-dotted band, and among commuters he looked surprisingly like just another one. His suit was wrinkled and he carried a briefcase and a roll of architectural, onion-skin drawings under his arm. He was sweating and seemed distracted.

Halfway down the platform we said good-bye to the cook and the maid who were going further forward to the coaches where they would ride sitting up. Although both had been with us since before my birth their flowered dresses and little church-going hats and their cheap, strapped suitcases made them strangers under the floodlights. Their pale, Irish faces were flushed.

There were four bunks in our compartment and my sisters and I argued over who should have which, where to put the suitcases, and what we needed for the night. "Make up your minds, for God's sake," my father said in a familiar tone that made me feel spiritless and sickly cool.

We turned out our lights as the train was clicking uptown through the tunnel. As it came out onto the elevated tracks, I was peering around the shade to see the people in the lighted Harlem windows. We stopped at 125th Street and when we were moving again and had picked up blurring speed I got under the covers. My father's reading light was on and he was lying on his bunk in his undershorts, smoking, with a closed book on his chest. My sisters seemed to be asleep.

There was a loud rap on the door and a shout from the corridor, "Tickets!" My father twitched violently, then ground out his cigarette and swung off the bunk. He yanked open the door, reached out and dragged in the conductor by the lapels with both hands and slammed his back against the wall. "How dare you wake my children!" in a hoarse whisper. The conductor's jowls jiggled as he babbled something. His hat and his gold-rimmed glasses had been knocked askew. "How dare you!" My father pulled him away from the wall and marched him backward out into the corridor, then reached back for the tickets in his coat pocket and waited, speaking in a low, dangerous voice, until the conductor had handed in the stubs. He closed the door and sat down on his bunk. His face was glistening with sweat and his hands trembled lighting a cigarette.

Above me Sage asked sleepily, but urgently, "What is it?"

"Never mind," he said. "Go back to sleep."

.　　.　　.

My father's royal blue Packard convertible was parked at the Rockland station. He had driven up to North Haven the weekend before and had returned by train. He put the top down and opened the rumble seat and we crowded into it with our suitcases on our knees and drove to the ferry. It was a startlingly bright day and the clangs and dongs of the bell buoys carried far over the blue-black water, glittering under a light breeze. When we neared North Haven the white wooden houses on the almost treeless hillside were minutely detailed—shadows under the clapboards and spots of shine on brass door knockers and knobs.

Our house was on the flat, north side of the island, a fixed up farmhouse reached by rocky roads and surrounded by stone-walled, but abandoned, hayfields. The barn had been made into a summer living room. A swing had been hung from one of the rafters, a Ping-Pong table had been set up, and my father's phonograph was ready to play. The barn doors slid open onto a long view of Penobscot Bay and the mountains behind Camden, and just outside was a patch of grass which Sage used when she did her dance exercises. Encouraged by my father, she had recently made up her mind to become a dancer and was working hard to catch up with the others who had started younger. In a gym suit, totally concentrating, she stretched and split and assumed ballet positions during the long practice periods that she had set for herself, and at every other odd moment. When he talked about our futures my father stressed "professionalism": the necessity of being truly professional at whatever we did.

My father read a great deal, several books at a time. He would drive Sage and me into the yacht club where he had rented a dinghy for us and I would sail it very badly. I rammed other boats at their moorings, capsizing more than once, and in the races came in last or near it. Sometimes Sage would take the tiller, but she did little better. We had had no instruction and, being newcomers, we were not much helped by other children. My father would meet us at the dock, coming in, and we would go home and play records, "Gloomy Sunday" and my father's collection of jaunty French songs, and sleep in the heavy, cold nights.

The township was legally dry although "real" prohibition had ended five years before, and I once went with my father to the bootlegger. His small, badly weathered house was about halfway between ours and the village, set off by itself near a little cove. "Mornin'," he said curtly when he answered my father's knock. He was a wizened old man and wore a watch cap.

"Good morning," my father said, smiling. "I understand from Mr. Felton that you have supplies of something I might be interested in."

The bootlegger did not smile back. "Will ya come in." The walls of his kitchen were covered with pictures of girls cut from Sunday color sections, most of them badly faded, and the place smelled old and sour.

"I'm happy to have found you. Happy to know you're here," my father chuckled.

"Will ya sit down." The bootlegger perched on a crate and stared at us.

"That's a pretty little cove down there," my father said.

"Ya don't mind the boy?"

"No no."

"Ya keep your mouth shut, sonny?" I nodded. "You, too, Mister?"

"Oh, sure," my father said.

We left with a case of beer, the only kind of drink he had just then.

Nothing noticeable happened.

One evening my father led us three children down to the rocky shore nearest our house and we built a fire and steamed clams and lobster in a bed of seaweed. He looked tremendously healthy, tanned, with the sleeves of a sweater tied around his neck. As the light dimmed on the bleached rocks and night fell we sang songs and laughed. He was very happy and sang Harvard's "With Crimson in Triumph Flashing" and funny things from his Navy days in World War I. Jill fell asleep and when the fire got to embers he carried her up to the house while Sage and I dragged the blankets after him, still singing.

Three days before we were to go home he told us that he was going to visit a playwright friend whom we knew, who owned a small island off Vinal Haven. He would be back to put Jill and the cook and maid on the ferry. They were taking the train and

Sage and I were to drive home with him the day following. He left and, during his absence, Sage and I exchanged not a word about him.

We could not get to town, but we did not mind. We were looked after and for the first time in the summer Sage and I paid attention to Jill. We went walking along the shore skipping rocks and trying to climb the hard places, showing off for her, and at home we played Parchesi together. Sage taught her dance steps to record music.

My father returned on schedule—drunk, the Packard skidding to a dusty, scraping stop. From his exuberant expression it seemed he had brought back a supply. "Hi! How is everybody? Everything all right? All ready to go?"

Sage said, "We aren't going till tomorrow are we?"

"Absolutely right! But there's nothing like being forehanded, is there? *God*, those islands are beautiful!"

He took his bag into his bedroom and I heard the snaps click open and a bottle being set down on the dresser. Sage followed him and they spoke in low voices. He said quietly, but distinctly, "I've been good all summer, haven't I? This is the first time all summer." After a silence, he enunciated, "And I'm going to have a drink."

I went over to the barn and played some music and looked around for things I might have forgotten. After a time the maid came out the front door wearing her traveling clothes, hat on her head, and waited restlessly. Her mouth was hard-set. Then my father appeared smiling his nothing-to-worry-about, aren't-I-pleasing smile which almost immediately vanished. He looked increasingly angry, but she went on shaking her head. The situation must have been painful for her; she was very sentimental about my father. Then he slammed inside and the cook brought the bags out, and Jill. They waited together in a bit of shade and after a while a taxi drove up, the only island taxi, and I went over to say good-bye. Sage came out, too.

The maid and the cook were silent. The maid did not want to say that she had refused to ride in the car with my father, and Sage and I were silent because we knew she had. Jill looked small and sad, her mouth drawn into a little ball. I envied her so much I felt like crying.

Sage and I had little to do for the remainder of the day. My father was at his desk in his room with a book, but he was drinking. Toward sunset he went for a walk, brief and alone. Sage and I ate something the cook had prepared before leaving and went to bed early.

"All right," my father said. The car was packed and the house closed. He was wearing a fedora hat. His cheeks were sunken in under his cheekbones, his lips were pursed—it was a particular look he had at these times. We reached the ferry without trouble. The sky was overcast and the white hulls of the sailboats moored at North Haven looked wintry on the dark water as we left them behind.

When we landed at Rockland, Sage was given the road map and we headed for Port Clyde down the coast, where we would meet Aunt Clarkie, my father's sister. We rarely saw her since she lived in Wisconsin, but her Christmas presents—ingenious, useful things for unexpected purposes—had made her a nice person in my mind.

Some miles along the highway Sage said, "I have to stop."

"All right." My father glanced at his watch. "It's about lunchtime, we'll stop."

We passed several places that offered food and Sage began to ask why not here?

"I didn't like the look of it. Did you, Blair?"

She said, "I've got to stop, Pa."

"All *right.*"

We stopped at a roadhouse and Sage rushed off to find the bathroom.

"Sorry, Mister, we don't have the license."

He reddened. Wouldn't the owner have a supply of his own, perhaps? "I'd certainly be glad to pay for it."

The woman went out to the kitchen and returned to say she was sorry, the proprietor didn't drink, there was nothing. Sage heard the last of this, sitting down beside me. When the woman had gone—could someone be sent out?—Sage leaned across the table and whispered to my father.

He sat back. "That's the situation, is it? Well. Let's see. Which one of us will go and get the Kotex?"

Silence.

"This is a democracy, isn't it? Who shall we elect?" He grinned suddenly. "What is your vote, Sage?"

Silence.

"Blair."

Silence.

"No votes." Then he said slowly, "Eeny meeny miney mo. Blair will go and get the Kotex. You'll do that for your dear sister, won't you, Blair?"

"No, I won't." At that time woman whispered their orders for "napkins" to druggists, and the boxes, kept behind the counter, were wrapped in plain brown paper.

"You won't help out your *sister*?"

"I don't know where a drugstore is."

"There are always drugstores, everywhere."

"No, I won't."

Sage leaned close to me, but I wouldn't look at her. She said, "I've got to have some. Couldn't you?"

"But where?"

When our attention went back to my father he stopped smiling and became "judicious." "Sage and I have elected you the one to get the Kotex."

"I won't."

It went on, Sage and I becoming angrier at one another. He interrupted by slapping the table so hard it jumped. "All right, *I'll* get it. Wait here." He left, aggrieved.

He was gone for I don't know how long, maybe two hours. Meanwhile, the waitress, pitying Sage's tears, had solved the physical emergency. At one moment Sage and I discussed eating to pass the time, but we had no money and did not dare order. We did not speak much and I knew that she truly hated me, at times, not because I had refused to go but because my refusal had sent our father out.

He came back very drunk. "*There,*" he said, chucking the brown box on the table. "Satisfied?" he said to me. "Drugstore's just up the road. No distance at all." He sat down, joined his hands on the table in front of him and looked up at us from under the brim of his fedora. He was someone new. "Have you eaten? Had lunch?"

We shook our heads.

"How about...*poulet roti normandine,* or, say, *scallopini Pisano*? The establishment would be honored by your choice, my children." He shook and coughed with laughter.

"I'm not hungry," I said.

"Then let us go on to Clarkie." he got up, lurched and grabbed the chair's back, then went to the door.

Sage whispered to me, "I won't go with him. Don't you either."

On the porch outside she told him she refused to go. "Of course you will," he said. "Get in the car."

"I won't."

I stood on one side hearing the pitches of their voices, his changes of tactics, her weakenings and firmings. Then I walked down to the car parked on the far side of the street, against the traffic, and got in. I thought that if I could get with him to Aunt Clarkie that she must see and stop it. She was his older sister. Then Sage could be found somehow. I looked around to fix the name of the roadhouse in my memory and saw a red-haired man crossing the street to me. He leaned on the window and said, "That your father on the porch there? He is, ain't he? Your father?"

"Yes."

"Yeh, well. I believe that man's been drinking, ain't he? Been drinking a whole lot, I'd say. My advice is, put him in a hotel and let him sleep it off. Don't drive nowheres. I wouldn't."

I nodded.

"That's the best thing for him, I'd say."

"What hotel?"

"There's one a mile or two back on the highway. Big old place, you couldn't miss it."

"Thank you."

"That's my advice," he said. He went back to the roadhouse skirting the argument on the porch. My father held out his arms to Sage and beckoned, then punched his fists into his hips. Sage stood still. He turned away, staggered, saying something to her over his shoulder, nearly fell down the steps, and came across to the car enraged.

"All right," my father said. "You and I'll do it. Your sister can stay here and think it over."

"What'll she do?"

He raced the motor, ground the gears into first and we jolted forward.

The two-lane highway wound sharply along the rocky coast. We would head straight for a telephone pole then jerk past it at the last second and head straight for the sea. Often the median line was visible beside my window—I was looking out it not to look ahead. There was almost no traffic, but one car, coming the other way, braked to a stop on the narrow shoulder over the water, honking, and its driver screamed with furious terror while my father, who had braked, too, wheeled around him to the right, laughing. Safely out of earshot, my father's face looked shocked.

We came to a village sign, Port Clyde, and my father stopped the car, turned off the ignition, and breathed deeply. The car ticked with heat in the silence. "I have some directions," he said, his voice quite different, soft and slurry. He fished a paper from his pocket. "Can you read it?"

"Yes."

He turned the mirror to look at himself and smoothed his hair and curled his lip to see his teeth. "You read and I'll follow the directions." We went slowly through the narrow streets. I missed one turn and he had to back up, and he snapped at me, "Do your job, for God's sake."

We stopped beside a grassy yard before a low white house, and Aunt Clarkie appeared through an open barn door toward the rear, dressed as I remembered her in a man's suit with her hair cut short. Behind her was Cousin Alfred. They both were smiling broadly. I sat still while my father hugged Clarkie and shook Alfred's hand. The three of them spoke and laughed at once. My father looked back and waved impatiently for me to join them and I got out and shook hands. The friendly things they said sounded like barking.

As I followed them through the barn door into Alfred's studio my father was being extremely interested in Clarkie and Alfred, surprised and fascinated by what they said. I remembered his doing this before. If he made other people think about themselves they would not see him. "Don't you think so, Clarkie?" I could hear the slur, but she was concentrating on the expression of her opinion and if she heard it too, it only made her more insistent on getting what she had to say across. She repeated herself several times. Clarkie and Alfred had half-full drinks sitting on the coffee table.

A very large, realistic painting of a stormy sea was standing on an easel. My father took time looking at it from one angle and then another, close to it and then from the furthest point in the room. "Wonderful, Alfred! Just wonderful. It seems to me you've made great strides since the last time I saw your work. The light there near the horizon..." He shook his head admiring it. It was the kind of painting I knew my father despised.

Alfred was glad my father had noticed the light near the horizon and had a lot to say about it. "Won't you have a drink, Chas?"

"Just a light scotch, if you have it."

"Nothing easier."

My father turned away from the painting toward the open doorway and I could see that for some moments he was glassily drunk. Then he shrugged his shoulders, sat down in a dim corner of the couch and asked them about distant relatives. He made them laugh at me, ramming other dinghies at North Haven. His speech slowed down after a while. "Time to go. Don't you think so, Clarkie?"

Clarkie's car was a huge black "touring" Chrysler, crammed inside with bags and household things. She would spend the night with us on the road and then head for Wisconsin. She had her hands on its door when she laughed suddenly and asked, "But where is *Sage*?" He went over to her and spoke in a voice I could not hear. She looked surprised, but nodded.

If I went over to them I could say that I wanted to ride with her to see what it was like, the big Chrysler, and then tell her what had been happening. But, no, I could not. I could not talk to anyone about my father except, sometimes, to Sage.

One Friday afternoon during the winter I had been sent in on the train from Mount Kisco to spend the weekend with him, and he had not been waiting for me at the Grand Central gate. I had stayed there fifteen or twenty minutes and then had picked up my overnight bag and gone into the newsreel theater, thinking I would spend the night there.

I did not want to try to telephone him if he was not able to meet the train.

I had watched the newsreels of number of times and had fallen asleep, but had been woken up and shown the door when the theater had closed at midnight. After some minutes of sleepy lostness I had gone to the waiting room and had again fallen asleep and again been woken up, this time by a janitor. He had told me that if I were lost I should go to the police. I had not liked the mention of police, they would obviously have called one of my parents, and I had left the waiting room and wandered in the station until a lunch counter opened. I had stayed there until I boarded the 8:45 train.

My plan had been to call my mother from the Mount Kisco station and to say that I had told my father I wanted to go ice-skating that day and that he had put me on the train. Would she believe that he had gotten up that early? It had appeared to be thawing, too. Would she notice? But when I did call there had been no point in telling my story. My father had phoned her the night before and they both had been "worried sick." By the time the chauffeur had come for me and got me to the house I had decided that there was no way around telling the truth about my night in Grand Central, but that I would not explain why I had not called. I preferred to be thought stupid or irresponsible. The next time I saw my father he was angry at me. My disappearance had embarrassed him. He had got to the gate just after I had left it, he said.

Now I could see that if I went with Clarkie I would have to answer questions. My father seemed soberer now and perhaps it would not be so dangerous.

In fact, he drove much better. The trip back to the roadhouse was astonishingly short. Clarkie pulled up behind us and she and my father walked across together to find Sage. She came out on the porch and I stood below it while they talked, Clarkie doing most of it. Clarkie treated the situation as a family squabble. Sage had got mad at my father for some obscure reason and he had lost his temper and had left her. Now we were all back together and everything would be all right. Sage was stubbornly silent for a time. Her face gets pinched in anger. Her eyebrows close down and her lips go white. My father stood aside, blandly listening. Clarkie said, "It isn't far. We won't go far tonight." And Sage agreed to come, with Clarkie.

We ate supper at a seafood restaurant on the highway. Clarkie and my father had several drinks to start. It was very hot in the place and the food was slow arriving. I could eat very little and the process was very long.

Afterwards, Sage got silently into the car with my father and me, and we drove further along Route One to "cabins"— motels did not yet exist. When we pulled safely into the parking lot the stars were out in the warm night. I had never felt so tired.

Sage and I got our shared overnight bag from the floor of the rumble which was open because the phonograph was sitting on the seat. "What shall we do with the record player?" my father asked. I did not understand what he meant. "Shall we leave it out overnight?" Silence. "Might it be stolen? Do you think it might rain?"

Sage and I looked dumbly at one another. He said, "It's up to you," smiling now. "Do you want to leave it or carry it inside?"

I said, "It won't rain."

"But someone might steal it," Sage said.

"Who'd steal it?"

"It's up to you," my father said. "The decision is yours alone." He was smiling more broadly now.

We argued. Since it would take both of us to carry it we must agree. My father stopped us and said he must have our votes. Sage voted to take it into our room and I voted to leave it out. Deadlock. The smile dropped from my father's face. "All right. Since you can't decide, there is just one way to settle this." He reached into the rumble, brought out the phonograph, and stepped backwards from the car. He swung it to one side, "One," swung it back, "two," and, "three!" threw it high into the air. It seemed to arc very slowly and then it fell and smashed apart on the asphalt. Parts tinkled, rolling away. "Now that's settled."

He walked away toward the cabins and Sage and I went to look at the wreckage. The wooden cabinet had split and collapsed and pieces were spread wide. Sage said, "*Why* wouldn't you carry it?" Her eyes were full of tears.

When we followed him he was standing in a cabin doorway holding a bottle in a paper bag. He pointed to another door and said, "Go to bed now. It's a long time since I've seen Clarkie and we're going to have a few drinks. Good night, now."

Sage and I did not speak before we slept.

In the morning he was red-eyed and shaky. He nipped. I could smell the whiskey. We said good-bye to Clarkie in the parking lot. She did not look so well herself and was fussed about all the things in the car and preoccupied with her long trip to Madison.

The day was crisp and sunny and we started for Boston with the top down. Sage sat next to my father. I did not pay attention to what they were saying until, after quite a few miles, he pulled the car over to the shoulder and stopped. "All right," he said angrily to Sage, "you drive, you know so much about it. You're going to drive the car." He got out, slamming the door, and so did I so he could sit beside her.

He told her where the seat adjustment lever was and then about starting, and the clutch and gears, to some of which she said, "I know." When she had started the motor his mood changed. "Off we go!" he said and laughed. The gears ground and the car bucked getting onto the highway but he never stopped smiling. Soon I was smiling, too. She drove for many miles, stopping at the traffic lights and starting again, staying in her lane correctly, and even passing other cars when he told her. "Now, go!" She frowned at the road ahead, gripping the wheel so closely that her back did not touch the seat, and she did everything right!

He told her to pull to the roadside and stop and she did so, and although he was smiling broadly, I could see from her face that she wondered why she'd done wrong. "Now it's Blair's turn," my father said. "Fair's fair." He laughed tremendously, coughing and having to wipe his eyes. Since I had not moved, he said, "You want to, don't you? Drive the car?"

"Sure."

"All right, then, what are you waiting for? Switch places."

The seat had already been moved as far forward as it would go. Some sweaters and other loose things were piled on the seat for me to sit on. I listened to the instructions and I started.

I could drive, too! I went at the right speed and stayed on the right hand side and even passed other cars, which threw my father into laughing fits. I made no mistakes and when he finally stopped me at a roadhouse, where he had several beers and we ate, I felt immensely proud and excited. Sage did not look happy but that did not damp my feelings.

He took the wheel through Portland and he did again through other large towns, but most of the day either Sage or I were driving and he was grinning away beside us under his fedora hat. It was so strange I could not make an accountable experience of it in my mind. No one would believe the police had not stopped us.

He drove into Boston and to the Ritz Hotel. Our bags were taken to adjoining rooms—wonderfully quiet rooms with pale curtains, and silky coverlets on the beds. He ordered a bottle on the phone and told us to take baths, that we were going to dinner at the house of an old college friend. We were ready on time and he was wearing fresh clothes and a necktie. He looked over our appearance very critically before we started.

The house was in Brookline and his old friend had a wife and a son about Sage's age who was told to show us various things like his room and the Ping-Pong table in the basement, at which we took turns playing. We were not good company for him. The old friend, a heavy, red-faced tweedy man had had the martini shaker in his hand when he opened the door, and we heard it shaken several times.

Mrs. Old Friend called down the stairs that we should come up for dinner and we did, but her husband was pouring when we came into the living room. My father was already drunk. She went to the kitchen to tell the cook to hold dinner and came back to urge the men to drink up. Finally she said, "We've got to go in. It's burning up." She was jittery and wrung her hands.

Her husband said, "Go ahead and we'll be in, in a minute. You'll have a dividend, won't you Charlie, with me? Sure you will, you others go ahead."

"You bet," my father said.

We followed her into the dining room and sat where we were told, all three children on one side of the table. Didn't we like the soup? she asked. We said, very much, and a minute later she asked the same question.

When they came in, the host sat at one end of the table opposite his wife, and my father sat across from us. The light cast dark shadows across his face and his smile was strange. He looked at us one by one and then raised a finger and pointed down the line, "Three, grim, faces," he said, and chuckled.

I looked into my plate. I believe that Sage was weeping. When finally we were released from the table she and I managed to get together by ourselves. She said she would not get in the car with my father. She swore it.

"What can we do?" I asked.

"I don't know." We did not know where we were so we could not go out the door and walk.

Sage went to the hostess and told her. "*What?*" she shrieked, as though Sage had insulted her. "What?" she giggled in a hopeless way and called her husband. *What?* He couldn't believe it. Charlie had had a few, no more than himself, and was perfectly all right. Who in hell did we think we were, talking like that about our own father! One of the finest men alive! His loud voice brought my father into the hall, red and angry. But Sage stuck to it. And I said I wouldn't, either.

The old friend said that he had never heard of such a thing. What kind of children were we? This struck an owed-loyalty note in my father. He looked very sad for us. "You know how children are," he said, patting his old friend's back.

At last the host said that simply to show how absurd Sage's fears were he would follow us to the Ritz in his car. Although logically there was nothing to choose between them, Sage rode in with the host and I went with my father. We hopped a curb at one point but we got there safely and so did they. When Sage said good night to the host he shouted to my father, "She'll know better next time, won't she Charlie? She'll learn some manners. She'd better!"

We went up to the rooms. While Sage and I were getting into our pyjamas my father came in through the connecting door. He had taken off his shirt and was barefoot and had a glass of whiskey in his hand. He said quietly, slurrily, to Sage, "Sweetie, it's been a bad evening, I know. He was very rude to you, and you didn't deserve it. Come and sleep with me in my room. Let's make up."

"No," she said. "I'm going to sleep here."

They began to argue. I did not want to listen and went about brushing my teeth and washing my face, but the tones of their voices changed, although both of them kept low-key, and I stopped and went to the bathroom door to see them. His hands were on her shoulders and her face was cast down.

"Wouldn't you be happier?" he asked. When he was drinking and wanted something, he wheedled in a sugary way. She shook her head. "Are you sore at me?" He turned and held her against him with one arm. "I shouldn't have left you in that roadhouse, damn it!" He looked down at her and kissed her forehead. His eyes were glittering, partly still in anger, I thought. Suddenly memories flashed through my mind of his asking Sage and Jill to take their clothes off in front of him. He would ask them to turn this way and that and would admire their figures but would make comments about the length of their legs or their posture as though they were statues. Then in a jumbled rush, which parched my mouth, I saw the pictures that I had found in the night table beside his bed in his New York apartment one weekend night when he had gone out and, sleepless and bored, I had opened a drawer and found an old photograph album. The pictures were brown with age so that for a moment I thought they were of his childhood. The people in them wore turn-of-the-century clothes, when they wore any, and had hairdos and mustaches of that period. They were fucking in strange positions, most of them staring at the camera, or they were alone and showing off their genitals. One very young girl was sitting on a rock beach with her dress held up to her waist and holding a long stick in her cunt. Among other thoughts, I had wondered why the pictures were antique. Didn't my father like present-day women, and sex? Had this something to do with my parents' divorce? When my father had come home he had stumbled in the dark taking off his clothes. I had not budged when he got into the bed we shared—it was the only bed in the apartment. I had never spoken of the pictures to anyone.

Perhaps now I made a sound or moved. I had a momentary, blinding vision of myself hurtling across the room and hitting him like a football player. My father looked up at me, annoyed, and I felt hotly suffocated.

"Sweetie, do come on with me," he said.

"No." She shook her head in a very definite way and he turned his face away from her, toward nothing, and a burst of pain and regret came across it. He blinked slowly and his jaw sagged to one side as he gave up. After a moment he ran his finger under his eyes and then stared into a corner of the room, looking deeply frightened and alone, so much so that I had an impulse to go and touch him, and perhaps I did move again for his eyes closed and he shook his head like a dog shaking off water.

He said, "I'll say good night to you, then." He kissed her forehead and walked unsteadily through his door and shut it behind him.

She fell on the bed and muffled her face in the pillow and cried a very long time. She was, and is, a person of great courage and is not easily cast down. At that moment I scarcely understood her grief.

In the morning we set out again for home. He said to Sage— his voice was broken down now, "All right. If we take the secondary roads you can drive more. You'd like that, wouldn't you?"

She did not reply and I don't believe he noticed it. Just beyond Worcester she took the wheel.

I sat between them. My father had a pint in the glove compartment and took occasional swigs. He was no longer laughing or smiling. His back was braced against the door and he watched the road from under the pulled down brim of his hat. Around midday the bottle was empty and he threw it out the window and I heard it smash at the roadside. After that we stopped several times for beer.

Sage let me drive a part of the way. I was excited but my eyes seemed foggy and my back ached, and I was afraid of making a mistake and being arrested. I was glad to give it back to her.

Near Bedford he told her to stop and he got out and brushed off his clothes and then looked at himself in the mirror, just as he had before we had met Clarkie and Alfred. He was driving, and pretty well, when we began to pass familiar landmarks near home, the riding stable and Hockley's Garage. It seemed years since I had seen them.

We turned into the driveway and stopped in front. My father had designed the house and he paused before walking to the door, looking at it. It was large and formal, with cream stucco walls and dark shutters, and a slate, mansard roof, "traditional," although not of any one style. At its third-floor level there was a triangular frieze in which was mounted a sculpture head of a unicorn, done by my mother, with a golden horn and a gold sunburst around his neck. Below it, a rotunda shaded the front door which was of dark, oiled wood with a large silver knob exactly in its middle.

One Easter, when they had still been married, a party of my friends had come for an Easter egg hunt. It had rained and indoor games had been substituted. After my guests had gone home the rain had stopped, and I had been sent out to collect the hidden eggs. I had been standing in the drive with a half-full basket, hoping I could pretend there were no more to be found, when my father had come out the door, grinning. He had picked an egg from the basket, hefted it, and then pitched it at the doorknob, and then another. "Can you hit it?" he asked me, and I tried. Very quickly, hard-boiled eggs and bits of colored shells had speckled the door and the terrace around it. My mother's window had gone up and he had suddenly run off down the drive, laughing and shouting, "Come on!" to me, "Run!" But I had looked at her and him, and had not followed.

Now my mother walked into the dim hall to meet us, dressed in immaculate cool clothes, her heels clicking loudly on the floor. Sage said good-bye to my father and went upstairs "to unpack" and did not come down before he left. I would have, too, but my mother said, "Come and sit with us."

I followed them into the living room and they sat down on either side of the fireplace with its polished bronze cat andirons, also my mother's work, and me between them, but across the room in the window bay.

"Wouldn't you like something?" my mother asked. "What would be good? Some iced tea or coffee, a drink?"

"What I'd like's a beer," my father said. "I'm easing off."

I knew she knew what that meant, yet she asked no questions. She rang the bell and in a minute the maid came in wearing her summer dress uniform of a black silky material with lace at the neck and cuffs. She nodded grimly both to my father and me, and when he had brought the beer and iced tea she looked over my head out the window, her pale eyes perfectly blank.

My father and mother began to talk in a way that sounded like flirtation. Bits of news of other people and about what each had been doing. Almost natural. A year ago I had been sitting where he sat now and he had told me that my mother was in Reno getting a divorce.

"Why?"

I do not know what he answered. I had been totally surprised.

There had been guests for dinner, perhaps eight of them, and my father had not changed from his tennis clothes. The martini shaker had been crackling for a long time. When the maid announced dinner he had said to me, "Stay a minute here, please. I have something I want to tell you." He had asked the guests to go ahead of him and to start dinner, saying that he wanted to talk to me. The guests had glanced in such a way that I felt very uncomfortable. Then he had filled his glass and told me.

"Why?"

When I could hear him he was saying that people sometimes found it impossible to live together and believed that they would be happier apart. "I'm sure we will be happier apart." He was sitting with his elbows on his knees and his face was beaded with sweat. After a pause he had asked, "Do you have a question? Anything you'd like to know? You'll be living here with your mother, but you'll see me on holidays and weekends."

"Where?"

"You'll come to visit me in New York."

I had been told my mother was visiting a friend in Wyoming. "When is she coming back?"

"In ten days or so. I'll stay in the house until then. Don't you want to cry?"

"No." The suggestion had offended me.

"It might make you feel better."

"No."

"Would you like to be alone a minute?"

"Yes."

"Well, I'll go in now and join the others. You'll be all right?"

"Yes."

I had not wanted to walk into the hall with him. The door could be seen from the dining room. I had waited, hearing their voices and then a hush, and then their voices again, and laughter. The only other way to my room was to go outside and back in through the kitchen where there would be other people. I had remained hidden beside the door until the voices in the dining room seemed busy with each other and then had stepped around the corner and gone upstairs.

Sage had been visiting elsewhere for the night. I later learned that she already knew and had not been surprised. She had guessed where my mother was.

Jill had a governess at that time, a small, pretty woman in her twenties, and she had heard me come into my room. Although I would not tell her what I had been told she guessed and tried to comfort me. I had not been much comforted but I was grateful to her. Several days later she had been fired by my father, and would not tell me why. She blushed and was tight-lipped and angry. When I had asked him the reasons, what he said was clearly false.

Now he finished his beer and said that he must leave. He had to get on to the city. My mother and I got up and walked with him to the front door. She asked me if I wasn't going to thank him for the summer.

"Thank you, Pa," I said.

He leaned down and kissed my cheek. The whiskey smell was very strong.

My mother went back toward the living room and I stood inside the screen door to watch him go. The afternoon sun turned the screen a bright copper-yellow—it was first class, expensive screening, he had once explained to me. I could see him through it very plainly. The Packard started and hummed. It kicked up some gravel when he moved, and he drove fast out the drive, pulling up a dust cloud behind.

One morning, thirty-five years later, I called a doctor and told him that I could not stop drinking. I was drunk, sitting at the desk in my office-studio in San Francisco. I told him I felt I had to leave the city for a time to dry out and get well, that a couple of days in a hospital would not do it. He knew I had had a nearly fatal attack of pancreatitis, alcohol-caused, and should not drink at all. He said that he would make some arrangements and call back.

I poured some vodka into a coffee cup from the bottle which was hidden, usually, in my desk, and phoned my wife. She walked over from her gallery and sat with me. She was shocked, I believe, and frightened. I felt a leaden, vinegary despair.

The doctor arranged that I be picked up at home. I took a taxi there, poured a drink, and put some things in a suitcase. Then I waited what seemed an endless time, occasionally slopping vodka into my glass, until the doorbell rang.

The man who had come for me was sixty or more, meticulously groomed with a pin of some order or fraternity in his buttonhole. I asked him to wait a minute, went back to the bar for a last hefty belt which nearly made me vomit, and then went out with him to his car. When I'd got in he reached across my chest and pushed down the lock button. "There's a half-pint of bourbon in the glove compartment," he said. "In case you feel you need it during the trip." He started the car and we began to rock along.

Early in World War II, four years after the trip down from Maine, four years that had been all descent, my father had gone to a "farm" in Rhode Island for alcoholic treatment. The Navy had refused to reactivate the commission he had held as a pilot in World War I and I think the shame of that refusal had produced his decision. Perhaps, though, he had simply come to a despairing morning like my own. After some weeks he had returned sober to New York and then had gone to sea as an ordinary seaman on a merchant ship. He had continued to ship out until he injured his hand in 1944.

The six years following must have been the happiest of his life. He got a masters degree in City Planning from MIT. He remarried, and he and my stepmother bought a house in Stonington, Connecticut, and both found there a new center of work and interest. I saw him often while I was at Harvard and we became untrusting friends.

Then he began to drink again. He was less destructive, less dramatic and irresponsible, but his last ten years were not cheerful for himself or others. His health failed: bad emphysema, then strokes. He retired at fifty-six, spoke of himself as a person whose life had been of some minor historical interest, and died at sixty-one.

Well. Here I was being carried to "Rhode Island," Calistoga, California, in my case, the countryside blurring by me. From twenty on I had been a daily drinker and had lived with a ghostly fear of just this result. I had once told a friend that I did not understand myself. My father had scared me so, and so clearly shown me the risks, why was I drinking? My friend had said, "He scared you, but, still, you must have thought there was something in that bottle." Yes, and that something's power affected me as much as him, although where he had acted I mainly fantasized.

We were halfway to Calistoga before I opened the half-pint and took a slug. The bottle was empty before we arrived at Myrtledale, a converted old resort hotel with palms planted along its driveway and a long, shaded verandah. I stumbled up its steps and went into a dim lobby in which a number of others were sitting. I could not and did not wish to see them very clearly.

I registered and sat withdrawn in a dim corner. After an hour or so an aide, a former patient, gave me my first "hummer," a double shot of bourbon in water given to new arrivals over the first forty-eight hours to prevent the withdrawal dangers of convulsions and DTs. I picked up the glass with two hands to drink. Some of the others could not hold a glass and drank through straws while the aide held it. One could not keep the straw between his lips and the drink was poured into his open mouth.

That night the woman in the new-arrival room next to mine, rooms with no doors and barred windows, had DTs nonetheless. Her cries sounded tortured, in pain and terrified, and then exhausted and pathetic, then terrified again. An ambulance came and took her to a nearby clinic with medical staff—there is a better than ten percent chance of death from DTs. She returned two days later, a tiny Scottish woman with a shining, smiling face.

By then I was feeling tremendously relieved, as though I'd lost half my weight. It had happened at last. All right. No more unacknowledged suspense. Here I was among the alcoholics. I was an alcoholic. Survival must bring better things.

When my father died my mother telephoned me in Rome where I was temporarily living. She suggested that I need not return, that no one would expect me to come from so far. My sisters were on a Caribbean vacation, she said, and she had urged them to stay on there as long as possible.

I flew to New York and did what I could to ease the business of it for my stepmother. After the quite impersonal service at Saint James' I took her home. She had had the apartment before they married and it was almost entirely hers in personality. I stood for a time looking at the plain brown urn of his ashes standing on her dresser, hearing an electronic-sounding discord. Not all right. Not the manner (alone from a heart attack while he was hospitalized for rest and drying out), nor the moment of his death, nor his and my relationship when last I'd seen him, or ever, nor my feeling at that moment for his memory, shaded and spattered as it was with awareness of my inadequacy to have made him well, guilt for his recent neglect, and resentment of his past uses and disparagement of me.

During his last drinking years I had been the most faithful of his children. He had hurt Sage at the time of her first marriage by so insulting her husband that her later divorce and remarriage did not change her feeling. Jill avoided him. I had gone to doctors, to an AA meeting, to his friends attempting to find something helpful to him, and I was the last person who should have done so. He was not going to accede to anything serious coming from me. One evening, in other company, he told me I was the least "bright," the least "interesting," in fact, the least of his children.

It may be that his appraisal of me had to do with my attempts to help. It may as certainly be that my attempts to help had to do with his appraisal of me.

He had never lost a childlike joy in being "bad," meaning unexpectedly destructive, an applecart upsetter. Drunk, he liked to recount wild insults and dangerous pranks, and when he did so his eyes glittered. But he could not be "bad" without whiskey. My help would have ordered his life.

I, on the other hand, wanted others to think of me as "good," a good person, responsible and sensitive. Thus I had to try to get him well. I failed, but even had I succeeded, I could not believe myself to be "good" without whiskey.

Perhaps he and I were both alcoholics before we ever had a drink. But alcoholics, like other people when they drink, find the effects they want in it.

Three years have now passed since I left Myrtledale. In that time I have almost never felt the urge to drink and, until now, the urges have quickly passed. It has turned out that, sober, I can like myself. Not too much, I think, just sufficiently. Perhaps the act of giving up the stuff has provided enough feeling of goodness to satisfy that vanity. I have a son, soon to be eleven.

In principle, of course, my father could have been more intentionally, cleverly bad without whiskey, but in fact he was not. He was at least as good as most men, sympathetic, understanding, and generous. Without the help of the drug he could scarcely be bad at all. Simply, he could not accept his own goodness (or mine), any more than I could accept my own badness (or his).

So, let me try the phrase in a different tone. All right, Charles Fuller. Finished. All right.

All right.

EDUCATION
IN GOTHAM

Under the greenish skies of New York's July evenings
Robinson Grant would walk up Sixty-third Street toward
his family's brownstone house carrying a quart of beer bought
coming from the subway. Although it warmed with every minute
he took his time, looking in the faces of those he passed and at
the dogs being walked, saying hello to the superintendents that
he knew and to his neighbors', the Fieldstones', chauffeur who
was usually standing beside Mr. Fieldstone's gray Imperial
limousine or her convertible, powder blue Cadillac. He would
glance through the archway and up the flagstone walk to the
coach lamps marking the Fieldstones' front door which—a
curiosity in New York—faced the side of the Grants' house rather
than the street. Lately, when they passed on the sidewalk, Mrs.
Fieldstone's eye seemed provocatively amused, as though she
were tempted to share a joke with him. Having seen her or not,
Robinson would then climb his steps, let himself in, and go up
past sheet-draped furniture to his room on the third floor. He

would raise the venetian blinds and pour himself a glass of beer, strip, shower, and sit near the open window in his shorts until the bottle was empty. Then he would dress again, go out for dinner at one of the cheaper restaurants on Second Avenue, and return to his room and the window, often with a second quart, and try to absorb the books on economics that the office recommended to him. But he found it difficult to concentrate.

Why hadn't he stayed out on the Island and had a good time as most of his friends were doing? He knew the answer well enough. Last summer the old amusements of sailing, social tennis, clambakes, and beer busts had bored him and made him feel unnaturally childish. But since he was, after all, sacrificing one of his last two summers before his Amherst graduation, and a lifetime of work, it was maddening that his job was not really a job at all. His father had made it sound genuine enough. "I know this fellow, Robbie, think he's a nice fellow, too, but I don't know him well. Done a little business with him, that's all. So if you get the job it'll be on your own merits." But from the very first Robinson had sensed that the regular force considered him superfluous and, in a way he had not immediately understood, privileged. They made work for him or asked him to make it for himself. "Would you like to go over the such and such?" He had discovered only last week that Barnes & Caldwell exchanged services with Hill, White, and Minton, his father's firm, in cities where one or the other did not maintain offices.

Sitting by the window Robinson often dropped his book, turned off the reading lamp, and, putting his bare feet on the sill, stared out at the lit windows across the backyards. To see people washing dishes, appearing as shadows behind translucent bathroom glass, watching television, gave him mixed sensations of sympathy and envy and fear. They appeared so contained, so heedless of everything but the job in front of them or their wives' voices or the book in hand. He envied their busyness and contentment but it seemed a little sad to him that people could be satisfied in such small spaces with so few familiar objects, year after year, and he feared that he too would accept a similar containment as his fortune and his life. He preferred the very different spectacle of the Fieldstones' house. Here all life was hidden, its noises drowned in the hum of air conditioners and its sights blocked off by curtains of bright, pastel shades. He was free to imagine, or almost. His mother and father had gone for drinks there once and his mother had described it afterwards as, "Very posh." The Fieldstones had never been invited by the Grants. Mrs. Fieldstone, with her complicated hairdos of bright blond hair and clinking jewelry, was not the kind of woman his mother liked. Indeed, she said Mrs. Fieldstone was "tough" which was just about the ultimate in her vocabulary of disapproval.

She did not look tough to Robinson. Her brown eyes were liquid and deep and she was normally made up, not painted. Only her mouth was slightly strange, wide and absolutely straight, the upper and lower lips inhumanly identical. Mr. Fieldstone was more clearly a type, although of exactly what, Robinson was unsure. Homburg hat, thick black rims on his glasses, briefcase and furled umbrella—what had his father said? Finance? Textiles? What was happening behind the pastel curtains? The Fieldstones went out quite often, but rarely had guests.

Robinson went to bed, not from tiredness but by the clock. If he had had a second quart of beer he would sometimes pose before the bathroom mirror, flexing the long muscles under his untanned skin, combing his lank dark hair, sucking in his cheeks to outline his strong cheekbones and jawline, and glaring at himself, head cocked to one side.

One evening early in August the blue Cadillac's top was down and the chauffeur was nowhere to be seen. Robinson climbed his steps looking over his shoulder at its golden, satiny upholstery. He had opened his beer and stripped to the waist when the telephone rang downstairs.

"Hello."

"Mr. Grant?" Although he had never heard her speak he knew that this was Mrs. Fieldstone.

"Yes."

"This is your next-door neighbor, Marcia Fieldstone."

"Oh. How are you?"

"Just fine. A few people are here for drinks and I thought perhaps you might like to join us."

"Thanks. With pleasure."

"Ours, I'm sure. Come any time. We're here."

As Robinson dressed, her voice sounded in his ears, smooth and modulated, not New York and not any other region that he recognized.

A butler, whose face was both icily correct and somewhat thuggish, answered Robinson's ring and led him through a short hall of black and gold furniture and silky fabrics, and showed him the several steps down into a room of leather, tan and deeper brown, with a bar at one end and sporting prints on the wall, in which the party was sitting. Mrs. Fieldstone uncurled from a couch and came to meet him wearing tight cotton slacks and a shirt tied under her bosom so that a triangle of midriff showed.

"Glad you could make it," she said, smiling. And to the others, "Here's my neighbor, Mr. Grant."

"Robinson Grant," he said, feeling himself blush.

"What a pretty name." She introduced him to the two other couples as Rob. He retained none of their names but recognized the face of a movie actor. Burt Rand, still young but not much seen recently. The women looked frankly in his eyes. All were dressed as casually as the hostess. No Mr. Fieldstone.

"Have you just come in from the country?" Robinson asked.

"Sherlock Holmes," said the actor.

"Joneses Beach," said one of the women, a very dark brunette with wine-colored lips. "I want to tell you, it was beautiful."

"I envy you," Robinson said.

The brunette nodded, blowing out smoke through pursed lips.

"We'll go another day," Mrs. Fieldstone said. "Maybe you'll come with us."

"I'd like to, but I work."

"No four-letter words, please," Burt Rand said.

"Would they miss you one little day?" Mrs. Fieldstone raised her chin and faintly smiled.

"Not too much, I guess."

"So it's settled." She made a gin and tonic for him and a scotch for Burt Rand—"Five fingers and don't drown it, honey."

Robinson sat down in one of the armchairs and the conversation flowed around him. They neither ignored him nor tried to include him, which would have been impossible since they talked mainly of mutual friends. Betty had gone out to the coast.

Herb was in Italy working on a tax deal for someone else. Robinson's eyes followed the voices in an effort not to stare. Burt Rand's shirt was loudly monogrammed; the other man's fingernails were lacquered. The brunette's cheek was dotted by two beauty spots; the second woman, a lanky redhead, wore an anklet with a small pendant in which a diamond glittered. Mrs. Fieldstone—Marcia, he corrected himself—was sitting in profile to him and was the easiest to study. Her toenails were an unfamiliar shade of silvery red; her teeth were very white and even, perhaps capped. Beside her wedding ring was a large, square-cut diamond; and on the little finger of her right hand was another diamond ring, less significant. But rather than richness the impression was of care, of showing to best advantage. The blond hair had been pinned up without a wisp escaping, the mouth perfectly applied. She held her head in such a way that Robinson saw the length of her neck. Her back was straight and shoulders squared so that the slopes of her breasts and the flatness of her stomach were apparent. It was an arrangement, but it seemed an effortless one.

After perhaps three quarters of an hour, Burt Rand clapped his hands and said, "We all had to start some time, didn't we?" Everyone laughed except Marcia who barely smiled and Robinson who smiled politely. "Got to cut now, kiddies," he said. "The rickshaw waits." He got up and the others followed. "Sorry you can't travel, honey," he said to Marcia.

She lifted one shoulder. "It'll blow over."

"When's he coming back?" the brunette asked.

"A week from Thursday. He *said.*"

"Life's too short," said the redhead.

"You can say it," said Burt Rand.

They were gracious to Robinson. "A pleasure." "Hope you'll come along to the beach some day." "Bye, for now."

When they had gone Robinson put down his glass and said, "I'd better be going myself. Thanks very—"

"Stay and have another," she interrupted. "Unless you have a date or something."

"Well." He glanced stagily on his watch.

"Go on," she said. "You're not going anywhere." And they both laughed. "Will you serve yourself and put a little scotch in this?"

"Sure."

When he had made the drinks she said, "Let's get out of this room. It gives me the creeps."

"Why?"

"It looks like the New York Athletic Club, or something. Anyway it's supposed to."

"Does your husband belong?"

"Ha!" And she truly laughed. "He's an athlete, all right. That Albert." Robinson followed her through the black and gold hall and an oval stairwell into a sitting room, all brilliant puffs of things, satin footstools and sculpted vermilion drapes and thick-piled white carpet and puffy cushions on the furniture, all multiplied by mirrors. "That was Albert," she said. "This is me."

"It's very pretty."

"But too much, hunh? Most people think so. Maybe I'm making up for the locker room, but I like it. Sit." She patted beside her on a love seat. "Your father is a very handsome man," she said.

"He keeps in good shape."

"Is that what he does? Sorry, honey, you're right, he does. They're away for the summer?"

Robinson nodded. "We have a house on the Island, near Huntington."

"That's the north shore, isn't it. Did you grow up out there?"

"Mostly." Her questions led him to describe his life as a boy, then on to college and now. He made another drink for each of them and felt quite mighty, holding her attention. Toward the bottom of his glass Robinson courageously proposed that they go out to dinner.

"I'd like to, honey, but unh unh."

"Why not?" He wasn't quite this naive but he wondered what she would say.

"Married ladies don't go out with young boys. This married lady doesn't go out at all. Ho hum." Her mouth did not appear to change and yet for a moment she looked bitter. "Would a sandwich be enough?"

"Sure."

"He could have a sandwich," she said to the air.

She ordered beer and sandwiches for two. They were of a kind Robinson associated with catered parties, thin sliced bread cut in triangles and clipped of crust, filled to every edge with delicate portions of food. When the butler left the room, Marcia closed—nearly closed—the door behind him. She was apparently amused watching Robinson eat. She merely nibbled. Finished, he sat back and was surprised by her fingers brushing the line of his jaw. "You're good looking, too," she said.

"You're beautiful."

"No," she said. "You're sweet but I'm not. I know what I've got."

"And what's that?"

"You know—what I've got. It isn't that good."

She had dropped her hand but had turned toward him in a way he thought inviting. He took her forearm and brought the hand back to his face. She smiled as he stroked his cheek with her knuckles, then drew away and stood up. "Fun's over. Now you're going to bed like a good little boy, and I'm going to bed like a very *good* little girl." She glanced at him, still sitting. "And no hurt looks, please. It's been simply grand, and now it's ended."

Getting up he said, "I was just surprised."

"A lot of things surprise you." She walked to the door, looked through it, and stepped back into the room. "Will you do me a favor? No shortcuts, hunh? Go out to the street and in your front door. All right?"

"You're being—"

"Watched. You guessed it."

"How do you know?"

"Why talk about it? Mainly, I know Albert. Another thing: this is good-bye here, hunh? No jazz at the front door. There are servants."

"Absolutely."

She softened. "I'm grateful to you, really. You spared me most of a lonely evening, and you're a sweet boy."

"You spared me the same. I've enjoyed it."

"OK, we're quits. Now out."

He heard her lock the front door behind him as he started for the street, not looking but keeping his eyes open for the watcher. He saw no one likely. Inside his house the prospect of his room depressed him and he went, instead, into the living room, removed several dustcovers, and sat staring at the mahogany breakfronts, the dim Persian rug, and the leather-framed family photographs and antique pillboxes on the round, Victorian end table. Marcia excepted, how did these people live? The actor apart, what did they do? Were they all connected with the theater?

After an hour or so the phone rang.

"Hello."

"You there?"

"This is Rob. How are you."

"Lonely."

"Me too."

"Very lonely?"

"Lonely extremely."

"Me also. Ho hum."

"What to do?"

"I had a thought," she said, "but I don't know."

"What?"

"The gate in your backyard. Does it open?"

"It's locked but I could find the key, I think."

"Probably squeak like hell."

After a short silence he said, "I used to climb that wall as a kid."

"Yah? ... Somebody might call the cops about a second-story man."

"It's my backyard."

A pause. "Do you want to?"

"Very much."

Another pause. "If one of the servants wakes up, I'll have to call a cop."

"OK."

"You're taking a risk."

"So are you."

"It's the story of my life. You're sure?"

"Yes."

"OK, listen. I sent the servants to bed and they're behind the kitchen, they shouldn't hear. The front door will be open but no lights on. Keep going up the stairs to the top floor and turn left. Mine's the only door. Got it?"

He repeated the instructions.

"Wait a half hour or so, will you? And don't use the gate if it makes a racket. Don't wait too long."

Robinson sprang up the stairs to his room. Tennis shoes for silence. He got them on his feet, stood up, and tripped on the loose laces. He tied them. But if someone saw the sneakers he'd be certain Robinson was a burglar. He took them off. But if he had to jump the wall his landing on leather soles would make a crash. A lot of people wore tennis shoes in summer. He put them on again and trotted down to the kitchen.

He yanked out the drawers looking for the bunch of keys. When he found them they tinkled in his hand. Oil for the hinges. He remembered a can on the cellar steps. The cellar door was locked. He began trying the keys, lost his place in the bunch, and stood back and leaned against the stove collecting himself. If he couldn't get *this* door open! He started again and found it. Before, he had inserted the key wrong side up.

He flicked off the kitchen light and waited for his eyes to accustom to the darkness. Had a half an hour passed? He had forgotten to look at his watch after she called. Not yet, he decided, but the oil would need time to penetrate. He let himself out. Except for the humming air conditioners, the city seemed unnaturally still. He crossed the yard to the gate and, although the darkness made it difficult, located the latch and padlock and hinges. Plenty of time, plenty of time. He squirted oil into every aperture he could find, noticing, as he did so, that he had left his bedroom light on. He would have to go up and turn it off. Now. Did he have the right key? There were only several possibilities for a padlock. One fitted but he could not turn it. He dripped oil in the lock. Still, it wouldn't budge. He tried another key and the lock crunched open. He put a hand to the wall, breathing.

Upstairs, he caught a glimpse of his grimy hands and sweat-streaked face in the mirror, hastily washed, turned off the light and hurried down again. He paused a minute by the gate and looked up at the quiet windows, behind which people were watching television, drinking, and yawning, and his adventure seemed so improbable as to be impossible. But the latch was in his hand, cool rough metal.

The hinges groaned, not loudly. He drew the gate closed behind him and peered at the street and then at the dimly shining brass knocker and knob across the walk. He crossed the flagstones feeling in danger of toppling to either side, as from a tightrope.

The knob turned. The door opened inward with the faintest swish. He stepped inside and, as he turned to close it, his shoes squeaked on the floor. He remained rigid for some seconds, half expecting to be hit on the head or to see all the lights go on and Mr. Fieldstone at his elbow. Nothing happened. Through the buzzing in his ears, he heard a clock tick. He felt his way along the wall to the stairwell, walking on the balls of his feet. Some light filtered down from a skylight he could see when he had reached the stairs. He climbed on thick carpet, unconscious of any effort, and, standing at the top, his energy was so abundant he felt his next step might bump his head against the ceiling. On his left a crystal doorknob glinted. He reached it, thought of knocking and decided not. It opened silently onto the scene of an undreamt, because too fantastic, daydream. She was naked, standing before a full-length mirror on the wall facing him. She saw him in it and, as she turned, something moved on the black carpet at her feet—a black Persian cat who jumped to the lemon-colored satin coverlet of the vast bed.

She put a finger to her lips, walking toward him, and brushed past to shut the forgotten door. Only when she dug her nails in his shoulder and snickered, was the situation real.

"I didn't hear a thing," she whispered.

"No accidents."

She patted his cheek sharply. "I thought you were the type who'd be handy around the house." She turned away from him and went to the foot of the bed where she struck a pose, hands on hips, swinging a little from side to side. "Disappointed?"

"Beautiful," he managed.

"Not true, but you're sweet." She came back to him and ran her thumbs along the lines of his lowest ribs. His hands met in the cushiony small of her back. They kissed and he felt, against the firmness of her mouth, the trembling of his own jaw. "Easy, honey, easy."

The cat made room for them.

While he stumblingly discovered her she gracefully revealed him to himself. Her fingers found the hollows above his collarbones, the tapering ridges of muscle running from behind his shoulders down his sides, the soft skin inside his biceps, and showed him the slimness of his hips.

"Don't feel bad, hun. With me it never happens the first time." She tapped his chest. "I like you."

When she went to the bath, Robinson got up, too, and wandered in the room. He fingered the gold monogrammed equipment on the vanity table and looked at her photographs, almost all of them of herself. He stopped before the full-length mirror and examined his reflection, touching where she had touched. Then he turned off the light and carefully drew the curtain away from one side of the window. He looked down at the yard and across at his dark bedroom window, thanking his lucky stars he wasn't on its other side. He dropped the curtain when the bathroom door opened, admitting light. Marcia giggled.

"Albert caught me looking once."

"What?"

"Caught me looking at you in your window. See, hun," she took his hand and held it in both of hers, between her breasts. "I knew I'd like you. I even knew you liked beer." She giggled again. "Sometimes you'd turn your light out and I'd just see your toes on the sill. What were you thinking about?"

"You, partly."

"Just part of me? That's not nice."

"You and other things."

"You can forget those other things now." Her fingers brushed across his chest, circling under the pectoral muscles.

They made love again, more successfully, and at two o'clock Robinson dressed and retraced his steps to his house. He did it casually and perfectly, without an unnecessary sound.

That was Wednesday night. Thursday night at nine he came in from his dinner and sat down to watch television in the library near the phone. She was to call when the servants were safely in bed. Eleven chimed and eleven thirty. She had given him strict instructions never to call her. Quarter past twelve.

"Hello."

"Oh, hun. Some friends of Albert's turned up and I had to entertain them. They just left now."

"Damn them."

"You can say it. The creeps. Do you miss me?"

"I certainly do."

"You can't come over though, hun. The butler's still cleaning up downstairs."

"I could wait."

"You want to wait an hour? Aren't you sweet. But I'm kind of tired."

"Not *too* tired," Robinson said.

"Fresh! Well, if you're sure you want to, but it has to be a whole hour. Not any sooner."

This time she was stretched out like the Duchess of Alba, reading a thriller. She said, "There's something about you I like, you know that?" She motioned to him to come to her and when he stood beside the bed she kissed and gently bit his thigh through his trouser leg.

Tired as he was when he returned to his room he again considered his image in the mirror. It seemed to him that he was truly seeing himself for the first time, that he had somehow been blind to the shape of his torso and the planes of his face and unaware of the texture of his skin.

Next morning he telephoned the office, sick, and at eleven thirty he stood waiting on the corner of First Avenue and Eighty-second Street. The blue Cadillac's top was down and beside Marcia at the wheel were the actor, Burt Rand, and the redhead, Anita something. They drove out on Long Island and took the ferry to Ocean Beach. Marcia had the key to a friend's cottage there. They swam and ate the delicious lunch the Fieldstone kitchen had provided and afterwards Robinson and Marcia made love in the bedroom. The heat and wine imposed a new rhythm. A pause excited, a certain attack surprised, another was tender, and a third an expression of force. Their breath caught simultaneously in their throats. They quivered together for what seemed minutes. "The end," she sighed. "Oh, if living was all like that. If it could go on and on and on."

When they joined the others on the beach Burt said, "Have a nice dip?"

Robinson laughed but Marcia said, "Aren't you clever."

"How about it, baby?" Burt asked Anita. "Nice little dip?"

"What's this, all of a sudden, monkey glands?"

"You're for the cradle, too, eh?"

Robinson lay down and closed his eyes, his limp body welcoming the sun's impact. He heard only bits and pieces of the conversation:

Anita: "She got a nice little sports car. Did you see it?"

Marcia: "She deserved it. Did you ever see *him*?" And:

Anita: "Why do they all live in Scarsdale? What happens to their wives out there?"

Burt: "They're taking care of the Boy Scouts."

Later, they swam again and as they were drying Anita asked Robinson, "You any relation to Cary?"

"No," Robinson said. "I don't believe his real name is Grant. I read somewhere that it's Poole, a name like that."

"Couldn't you make it up? Couldn't you just pretend or something?"

"Leave him alone," Marcia said to her.

"Well, Jesus. Life's too short."

Back in the city, Robinson telephoned his mother to say he would not be coming out for the weekend. She sounded disappointed and tried to change his mind. "There's a dance at the Yacht Club tomorrow night." Robinson nearly laughed.

Later, in her room, Robinson taxed Marcia for defending him from Anita. "You didn't have to say that to her."

"You have it tough, all right," she said. "I know, I know, you can take care of yourself. But I know what she wants, and she isn't going to do that to me." The possessive note assuaged him.

They went to the beach both days of the weekend, Saturday with the brunette ("I want to tell you, this is gorgeous") and her friend, and Sunday with Burt and Anita again. With the others Robinson was almost entirely silent and with Marcia he found he had less and less to say. Politics and sports—common coins he could handle—did not interest them, and their knowledge of entertainments and show people was so much greater than his own that he had little to add. They spoke mostly of mutual acquaintances and while they often said things which amused him—"She had her nose fixed and it came out Mickey Mouse"—the wealth of characters and confusion of names was such that he often got bored. Saturday afternoon he listened to the ball game on the brunette's portable radio, and Sunday he took a long walk.

That evening, waiting for her call, it occurred to him that while her friends', and particularly Marcia's, company had brought his body into such focus that he was constantly aware of it, his personality had receded almost to absence. Her friends treated him as a piece of baggage, a mute pet, opening the door for him at Eighty-second Street and making room for him and depositing him there at the end of the day. And Marcia's recognition of him was almost entirely in love. When he touched her he became real to her and in a sense important, he was sure. "Oh, hun, you're *too* much." But when they were physically separated she seemed nearly as unconscious of him as her friends. Their lovemaking was so much more intimate than any he had experienced, and it so filled his life, that he could not believe she was as unaffected by it as she seemed.

He tried a few gambits, later on:

—"I major in philosophy."

"You read *those* things?"

—"I'm on the track squad up at Amherst."

"I'll say."

But Monday evening, waiting in the same chair, it seemed to him that her attitude contained a certain justice he should recognize. What was he? The son of a nice, conventional family, a junior in Amherst, who had never accomplished anything, never been in the newspapers, never married or divorced, or won the sweepstakes. What could he tell them that would fascinate them? Under the circumstances he should feel lucky that Marcia had been attracted at all, and lucky that his company was tolerable if not exciting.

That night was extraordinary.

Next afternoon Robinson climbed the stairs from the Fifty-ninth Street subway stop, tired and sticky with heat. Strolling to Sixty-third, he looked at the sky for signs of a thunder shower and in the shop windows for pretexts to stand still. When he turned his corner he saw Albert Fieldstone's gray limousine and the chauffeur standing beside it. For a moment his own shock surprised him, but then he remembered: today was Tuesday, not Thursday. The Cadillac was absent, Marcia had gone to the beach.

Robinson said, "Good evening," to the chauffeur and hurried into his house and to his room. A man, face invisible under a straw hat, was standing beside the Fieldstones' front door. After a few minutes, he left it and paced the walk, then returned and leaned against the house, arms folded. Slightly dizzy, sweat icy on his ribs, Robinson went to the front of the house and drew a chair to the window. Through the slats of the venetian blind, he could see most of the street and the sidewalk.

She was alone in the car. Perhaps she had seen the limousine from the end of the block for she drove up very slowly. Double-parked beside it, she sat a moment looking down the walk, then got out and threw the keys at the chauffeur. They fell to the sidewalk and he picked them up.

Robinson ran back to his bedroom.

The man tipped his hat to her and stepped in front of the door. Robinson could hear their voices; his even and definite, hers sharp but controlled, but not the words. She reached past him, presumably for the bell, and his arms swung out to each side of the entrance. She said something angry, tossed her head and walked away from him, then circled back. Now she gestured, slapping her fist into her palm. After a discussion he turned, still watching her, and rang the bell himself.

It opened only a few inches, clearly arrested by a chain. Words were exchanged and the door closed. Marcia was apparently satisfied for she now walked back and forth in silence, glancing once in Robinson's window. He was standing away from it, so she could not have seen him.

She was ten or fifteen feet from the door when it opened again and a fur coat was thrown through it onto the ground. She uttered what was nearly a roar, ran to the coat and picked it up.

"You jerk!" rang through the backyards, and she strode off toward the street.

There, she got the key from the chauffeur, slapped him hard on the cheek, jumped into her car, and drove away with the coat beside her.

Robinson lay on his bed, staring at the ceiling. He, Robinson Grant. Robinson Grant known as Robbie. Twenty years old, an Amherst junior.

After a time, he went downstairs and waited for her to call. It was past ten when it came.

"Don't say anything. Write down this number and go out and call it from a booth. Ask for Mrs. Park."

He called from a bar around the corner.

"Did you see it?"

"Yes, I—"

"He bugged the phone."

Robinson swallowed. "Had the phones tapped?"

"Albert's sweet," she said.

"My God. The one thing we didn't think of."

"It's the story of my life."

"Then he has—"

"Your name and address? I guess so, but don't worry, hun, it'll never get to court."

"If he has the evidence, why not?"

"I know a few things, too."

"What do you know?"

"Never mind what, for Christ's sake. Things he doesn't want to see in the *Daily News.*"

"But if he'll do something like this..."

"Listen," she said. "You've got worries."

"How are you?" he asked, penitent. "Where are you now?"

"Having a ball, what do you think? In a hotel."

"Can I come over?"

"What's the point? I haven't even got my equipment." She snickered. "Maybe I should have asked for it with the mink. Call me tomorrow when you get through work. From a booth."

"Why not from the house?"

"Maybe your phone's bugged. I'm still married to him, you know. It isn't over just like that."

Remembering the conversation, it seemed to Robinson that he had been selfish and boorish. She was the one who was suffering, not him. The following evening, when he went to her hotel, he was determined to make it up.

She was walking restlessly around the suite, wearing the same blouse and slacks she had had on returning from the beach. "Look at me," she said. "I've been talking to so many lawyers I haven't had time to buy a skirt. I can't even go out for a meal."

Robinson said, "Every time I think of it I get madder at him. Locking you out! Who does he think he is?"

"Yah, yah," she said, absently. "And I was a good little wife to him, too. Remember? I mean, let's face it."

"But you didn't treat him like a stray dog."

"So what's the difference? I knew Albert when I married him, hun. Or I guessed right. I only knew him three days when he proposed. What do you think of a man like that? He hardly knew me, didn't know a thing about me, and he proposes. I'd say he deserved what he got."

"Where did you meet him?"

"On the coast. Right away he asked me to go to Honolulu with him." She shrugged. "Why not? It's the story of my life."

Several people telephoned while they had drinks and dinner. "It's all right," she repeated. "He'll settle. No, I can't go anywhere. I haven't even got my face."

Robinson asked if Park was her maiden name.

"No, hun, my first husband's."

"Who was he?"

"A fellow. A nice boy."

"That's all? Just a nice boy?"

"We were very young. It was sweet." She shrugged. "But nothing, real nothing."

In bed, the dramatics of the last twenty-four hours were entirely forgotten. She was exactly as she had been and he as well.

Indeed, during the days that followed, Robinson had often to remind himself that a marriage had dissolved because of him, and that he was the correspondent in a potential divorce suit. For almost nothing had changed. He went to the office as usual. He returned with a quart of beer. The backyards looked as peaceful as ever from his window. He spent most of each night with Marcia. He no longer had to play a sneak thief to see her, and he walked around the block rather than risk encounters with Albert—those were the only differences. But, he told himself, they have evidence, my voice on tape. They will go to court over money. I'm the responsible party and I can't get off scot-free. Despite a number of "don't-worries" from Marcia he became increasingly certain that something would happen which would clearly implicate him. He dreaded it and partly wished for it to end the suspense.

One evening, some two weeks after the lockout, Robinson was in his room and about to step into the shower when the phone rang downstairs.

"Hello."

"Mr. Grant? Albert Fieldstone here."

Robinson forced a breath. "Hello, Mr. Fieldstone."

"Call me Albert, won't you. And your name is...Rob?"

"Robinson."

"Right. A few people are here for drinks and I wondered if you'd like to join us."

A dozen thoughts converged into a stammer. "Weh-well, thanks very much, uh, Albert, but...I'm not sure. I had a tentative engagement, but..."

"Just leave it open, Robinson. If you can make it, come any time."

Robinson sat back bewildered. Wasn't it clear from the tapes who her lover was? Or had Fieldstone been bluffing about the tapes? Or was he trying to trap Robinson somehow, to get an admission from him, or hand him a legal paper of some kind? Was the man a masochist?

He called Marcia. She was neither amused nor amazed. "Well, well, what's he after this time?"

"I've been trying to think."

"Want to do me a favor?"

"Sure."

"Go. There are a couple of things...but you wouldn't be much of a thief, would you. Not experienced in that line. Anyhow, go, and tell me later if you see the cat and how things look. What he's done to the place. He's probably been selling everything he gave me. If you can get a look into that downstairs sitting room, see if there's a little platinum cigarette box. It might fit in your pocket."

Robinson felt hysterical, dressing. First he'd stolen the wife, now he was supposed to rob the house. Robinson Grant.

The Pinkerton, sitting in a corner of the walk, glanced blankly at him. The thuggish butler was entirely passive as he undid the chain and opened wide the door. He led Robinson to the Athletic

Club bar from which came voices and a laugh. The faces were so reminiscent of those that had been there that first evening that Robinson felt unable to breathe for a moment, as in a bad dream. Albert Fieldstone, black shiny hair, black-rimmed glasses, heavy jaw, and brusque gestures got up to greet him. "Glad you could make it. How are you, Robinson?"

"Fine thanks."

"I'd like you to meet..."

The men played it straight enough but Robinson thought he saw amusement in the women's eyes. When he had completed the circle and was standing indecisively, looking for a chair, Albert put his hand on Robinson's shoulder and said loudly, "Robinson here did me a great service."

The room burst into laughter and, in his astonishment, Robinson laughed, too, realizing, crucial moments later, the complicity with Albert that his laughter implied. He straightened his face but there seemed no way to retract.

"So I thought he deserved a drink. Take a load off your feet, Robinson."

He sat down on a sofa next to a busty, feather-cut brunette.

"You're the most popular boy in town," she said.

"I don't see why."

"Oh, I do." She raised her eyebrows.

A half hour later, when he got up to go, he was held by her hand. "You can't *go*," she said. "You've got to take me to dinner."

"I'm afraid I have a date."

"Like, break it."

"I can't."

"You're no fun," she said. "I'm in the book. Ginny Sill."

Albert stood up to shake his hand. "I'll ring for the butler to let you out. Come again, any time. It's been a pleasure."

Finding himself alone in the hall, Robinson walked past the front door to Marcia's sitting room. A light was on. He scooped up the cigarette box and put it in his pocket. The hall was empty when he returned. He stood by the door, waiting for the butler, but instead Albert appeared from the bar, the butler behind him. Albert smiled, making the gimme sign with his fingers, and Robinson handed him the box.

■   ■   ■

"...He even had a girl lined up for me."

"Who?"

"Her name was Ginny Sill."

"You should have gone with her, she's cute. Got the cutest little fanny I ever saw." Marcia was pacing around the room.

"You would prefer me to have gone out with her?"

"I'm not the jealous type."

"I guess not."

She stopped and gave him a glance which seemed almost surprised that he was there. "I'm glad you didn't, hun. You're a sweet boy." She began walking again. "What's he after? What's he after?"

Robinson had not wanted to tell her about Albert's speech of thanks and their laughter, but she seemed so worried that he did so now.

"Well, thank God," she said. "It's that simple. Oh, you Albert. You clever jerk." Then she got angry. "Why didn't you tell me? I was worried sick, thinking he'd bought you off and I don't know what. Now it makes sense."

The episode of the cigarette box did not affect Albert's friendly manners. At one of their sidewalk meetings he said to Robinson. "I saw Ginny last night. She likes you. You ought to give her a call." The "injured" husband was pimping for him!

Robinson counted his advantages. He was sleeping with a beautiful woman. No one was trying to do him harm. Apparently his role in the separation was not going to be publicized, either in the newspapers or in court. And yet he became increasingly depressed, dragging himself through his day of work and sitting stonily with Marcia in the evenings. One night, a little drunk, he made what he knew, even while he made it, was an absurd scene.

She had been talking about the clothes and jewelry she expected Albert would sell off. Robinson said, "I certainly got you into a mess, didn't I?"

"It's not to worry, hun. It had to happen sometime. If it hadn't been you, it would have been someone else."

"You really don't give a damn about me, do you?"

"Well, you poor boy! He drinks my liquor, eats my food, we have an every night affair, and I don't like him enough. Poor Rob!"

"It's true," he said. "To you I'm just a piece of machinery. Useful to you. Useful to Albert. Useful to God knows who."

"You have it tough, all right. And I'm no use to you, I suppose? What do the good little boys from Huntington expect out of life? Oh, you have it tough, all right. You should have seen *me* ten years ago."

"But it's true," he repeated.

She turned away and shrugged. "Go on. Call up Ginny Sill."

He left and did so, and she had, indeed, a charming fanny but he never called her again. With her, too, he had the sensation of being personless—or a person entirely created by his affair with Marcia, a set of physical properties assumed to be pleasing. And for the first time the impression frightened him. Outside of the tiny circles of his family, Huntington, and college, was he this thing, this nothing? If he allowed himself to be treated as such, would he become it? He was in a kind of purgatory between what before he had thought himself to be, which he now knew to have been both a superficial and incomplete description, and a personality that was being thrust upon him which was a product of what these people wanted of him. Beyond the satisfaction of their needs, he was as superfluous as at his job. Robinson Grant, he said to himself, Rob-in-son Grant, vaguely hoping that a vision of himself would materialize.

After several days, he made up with Marcia. Through her the new personality had been made. It would not be extended.

"What happened?" she asked. "You didn't get along?"

Not long after the reconciliation, he arrived at her room one night to find a party going. "He signed the agreement, hun."

Everyone was congratulating her on its terms. Anita said, "Am I jealous!"

Burt to Anita: "I hear the Swedish Angel's in town. Want me to fix you up?"

The party moved up to a tower apartment on Central Park West and then to another apartment on Riverside Drive. Ginny Sill was there. "What's she got that I don't?" she sourly asked Robinson. "Except a wad of Albert's money." Robinson was late and hungover at work.

After that night he saw less of Marcia. She was often busy. It occurred to him that before the agreement had been signed she had had to limit herself to him. Albert already had the evidence on their affair, compounded at that, but any other affairs she might have had would have constituted new evidence and might have moved the legal balance in his favor.

During the evenings Robinson spent alone, he often stopped in front of his mirror. There were the hollows above his collarbones, the ridges of muscle running down his sides, the jawline she had admired. They felt foreign to his touch, as though they belonged to other men—which with very slight variations they did, he now realized. Only in an academic sense was Robinson Grant unique.

Albert remained friendly. One morning he asked confidingly, "What happened to you and Ginny? She's a good kid."

Robinson quit his job the tenth of September. His boss said congratulatory words to him which made Robinson secretly sneer. At the family dinner table in Huntington his father said, as Robinson knew he would, "I hope you learned something this summer, Robbie."

And Robinson answered, as he had prepared himself to do, "I think I did, Dad. A lot."

The last time he saw Marcia, before leaving for college, she said, "You're sweet, you know? Give us a bell when you get down from school."

Robinson tried to tell the story to his roommate but he quickly saw it was hopeless. The story, as it circulated in the fraternity house, told of Robinson Grant, Don Juan.

THE SCENT
OF WARMTH

Remington Knox fingered the slippery plastic wheel of his Citroen station wagon, the chemical new-car smell sweet to his nose. When the light turned and the car reared gently, starting to move, he said to the real estate agent beside him, "It's in Passy then."

"Passy, Auteuil," the agent shrugged. "I wouldn't know exactly where the dividing line's at."

The sixteenth *arrondissement*. How far away this richly respectable quarter had seemed to him seven years ago when, as a student, he had lived in a sixth-floor walk-up maid's room in a building behind the Pantheon!

From the backseat Frankie said, "It seems to me we're already miles from anything."

"Don't worry, ma'am," said the agent. "They're miles in the right direction."

"We're just going to have a look, Frank." Remington felt her fingers leave the back of his seat and imagined her faint but intense frown, and he was annoyed by her uncertainties.

"Let me see, now," the agent was peering nearsightedly through the windshield. "Rue de...slow up a little, will you? Rue de l'Assomption."

The name caught at Remington's memory and he glanced at the street, but saw two unfamiliar rows of apartment buildings.

"Rue de l'Assomption. Yeah, just a couple of blocks and you take a right on Rue Jasmin."

The building was new, the furniture ordinary, the apartment's "features" outstanding—washing machine, big refrigerator, second bedroom large enough for Jane, their daughter, to play in, nearness to the *Bois*. Everything they had been shown in more historic neighborhoods had had at least one serious drawback.

Frankie apologized for her eagerness. "If you don't like it, darling, please, please, say so. I know it isn't just what you looked forward to, but it seems to me..."

Remington would be spending most of his days in libraries or visiting the places most frequented by Flaubert, and that he would spend his nights in bland modern comfort did not disturb him at all. "What counts is you and Jane," he said. "I'll be perfectly comfortable."

They moved in next day and Remington set to work arranging his study. The card catalogue would sit on the desk, the typewriter to its side on a small, but sturdy, table. There was plenty of room on the shelves for his books and notebooks. Good light through the window which gave on the uninteresting and hence undistracting court. He would have the time now, and he was in the place, to do his somewhat overdue doctoral thesis. "The influence of Louise Colet's poetry and personality on Flaubert's conception of *Madame Bovary*." He could see it now, perfectly typed and discreetly bound. He could hear his voice, ironic but respectful, presenting the manuscript to the chairman of the department at Yale, "For your bedside." It was Remington's theory that Bovary was an inarticulate version of Flaubert's mistress. If Emma had taken pen in hand, wouldn't she have written:

Where, O where, are those divine souls
Whose thirsts are quenched only by Ideals?

And: My arms need arms, my soul needs another.
 Spent in solitude, beautiful evenings make me weep.

Tenable, Remington thought, perfectly tenable. Then he
smiled at himself. The thesis had been approved, that was what
counted.

That evening, Jane already in bed and Frankie in the kitchen
cooking their first meal at home, Remington sat on one of the
foamy sofas in the living room drinking whiskey. He had no
papers to correct, or lectures to prepare. A gentleman scholar was
he. With his thesis out of the way he could soon expect tenure
and promotion.

And Frankie. What a good idea it had been to marry Frankie!
He poured a third drink remembering their first meeting at a
party in Hartford. She had seemed *sauvage,* shy but with deeper
fears, and this had surprised him for she was good-looking,
although too thin, large brown eyes in a lightly freckled, heart-
shaped face. During their conversation her face had often
snapped away from him; he had lost the thread several times.
Someone there had told him that she was an only child whose
parents, New Yorkers, had been killed in an automobile accident
when she was eleven, and that a spinster great aunt had brought
her up in Hartford. Remington had been touched; his mother
had died when he was thirteen—if his father had gone, too? He
had called and taken her to dinner, then again a few weeks later,
then again. As her shyness receded (it was still there, even now)
he discovered that she had an odd, to him unique, quality. She
had the gift of making him participate admiringly in her battle
with self-pity. She would say, "I was born at a time, or at any rate
among people, where names weren't supposed to have a sex
anymore," and laugh, amused and yet determined to be. She
resented her name because it made her, an orphan, even stranger
to other children, and her resentment must be laughed at, to
complain would be unworthy, but the resentment was so strong
it could not be entirely hidden. When she told him about her
schooling or her work (she was then shuffling papers for one of

the insurance companies) there was often the same note of courage in the face of what she knew was her own weakness. He had been puzzled, then had sympathized, and had felt very solid through the middle beside her. But he was never allowed to express much sympathy. She possessed a wicked, embarrassed-at-itself sense of humor with which she cut him short. She often blushed at her own jokes which were usually at the expense of other people's motives. Behind closed doors it was the perfect sense of humor for academic life.

When they had begun making love Remington had been astonished by her nerve. Once her aunt had gone upstairs to bed it was as though there were no ears or eyes in the world except their own. She had gripped him in such a passion of possession that for a long time he could not tell whether she was truly enjoying it or not. But her possessiveness had stopped, surprisingly, once he had left her arms and the house. If he called to say that he could not get to Hartford according to plan, she would say, "Too bad," without a hint of reproach, and with never a question as to when she might see him again. He had supposed that her sudden nonchalance sprang from a kind of pride. Above all, she did not want him to feel indebted to her. Still, he had felt stirrings of jealousy, imagining a standby lover who contented her when he wasn't there.

One evening when he had picked her up, she had answered the bell already wearing her overcoat. "Good night, Aunt Pol," she had called inside and had skipped across the porch and run down the steps. She stopped halfway along the flagstones to the sidewalk and when he had caught up with her, she said, "I have an income of twenty thousand dollars a year." Amazed, he had laughed uncertainly, but she had not seemed at all disconcerted. "When my parents died, what they left was put into a trust fund for me, and Aunt Pol had the income reinvested until I was twenty-one." Then she had smiled suddenly and said, "Now I want to see a movie. A great big long Bible movie. Or a shoot-'em-up." This, too, was pride, he had thought. He was not to feel she was dependent and unfortunate; no pity should be spent on her on that account.

He had not been burningly in love with her the day they married—perhaps he had never been in love with her, exactly—

but he had been fascinated and touched. He had loved her strongly, as he did to this moment. The marriage had worked; it continued to work. Perhaps because she was an orphan she seemed willing to sacrifice more to make it do so than other women. She shared his worries and difficulties and put her own in second place. Her passion for him had lost its urgency but a shy tenderness had replaced it which suited him as well—better, for his ardor had weakened, too. And to watch her with Jane was a joy to him. What humor she found in the child! What pleasure in her games! He had hoped they would have a second child this spring in Paris.

And that income of hers...He hadn't had to scramble for another Fulbright or cut out whiskey for two years. He had had only to arrange to take his sabbatical a couple of years early and call the travel agent. Money wasn't everything—no one could attribute the contrary thought to a teacher—but much less so was poverty.

When Frankie called him to the table and he saw the candles lit and the bottle of *gros rouge* and the steak sizzling on the platter, he said, "Lovely."

"La la," she said, smiling and sitting down across from him. "Old Fitzgerald covers the earth."

He laughed and she grinned crookedly, and he remembered her Aunt Polly telling him how well Frankie looked, how marriage had improved her. And others, really startled, "But she's so pretty now, Rem." And she is, he thought. The stove had slightly flushed her cheeks and her eyes shone wetly in the candlelight. The fullness of her skin, which had been tight to her cheekbones when he had first met her, gave him a feeling of earned luxury.

"God, I'm glad to be here with you," he said, and she kissed the air in his direction.

Michele lived on Rue de l'Assomption! Remington had been searching in an old address book for a friend, a *Normalien*, whom he thought might be some help on Flaubert, and there she was, the Marseille address crossed out and the new one, copied from one of the few letters they had exchanged after his return to America—one of them announcing her divorce—written in below it. His immediate impulse was to pick up the phone, but the number was not there, and as he reached for the directory his hand stopped in midair. He had better think it over.

He did so off and on all day, in the metro and in the library, over coffee after his *quick service* lunch. Would Michele and Frankie like each other? It did not seem very probable. In the first place Frankie's French was not fluent enough for her really to know whether she liked anyone in that language, and more important, Michele possessed exactly that kind of physical confidence and force which invariably made Frankie uneasy. Still, it might be tried. How to introduce them? Had he ever mentioned Michele? Yes, my God, he had, not by name, but Frankie had teased him once about his love life in France and he had told her quite honestly that no, it had been an ascetic year except for several weeks on the Riviera. Who had been there? And, yes, he had supplied a few words of description.

On the metro going home he decided against the call. They would make new friends; why risk a complication? In any case, it only now occurred to him, he had probably been wasting his time thinking about it. Michele's last letter had arrived—was it *six* years ago? Almost undoubtedly she had either moved or married since.

Curiosity overcame him a week later. In the directory by streets he found Mme. M. Plas, 78, Rue de l'Assomption. He looked at the date on the directory—1978. If she were still there, he was almost bound to come across her in the street, and if it happened, he could bring her home and introduce her. If it didn't happen, *tant pis*, he would forget about it.

Which, for the next three months or so, he did. His work was going well and since he had done most of the reading in advance it was the pleasantest kind of work, visiting houses, restaurants, and hotels and taking notes on them; examining prints of Paris as it had been around 1850. He had already mapped out the chapters and believed that he could start writing after the New Year. They went to the theater twice a week, dining at different restaurants picked from the guidebooks beforehand, and often trying nightclubs after the final curtain. A reliable baby-sitter had been found and a woman who came in three days a week to clean. They made a few agreeable friends. It was Frankie's first visit to a foreign country but she was not at all dismayed by her difficulties with the language, customs, or suspicious of what was new to her.

And then... Was it Jane's whining with her colds? Or Frankie's inability to pronounce a French word with anything that resembled the proper accent? Was it the dankness of the Bibliotheque de l'Arsenal, or the rich-sick smell of the metro, the shortness of the days, the damp darkness collecting under heavy clouds at four in the afternoon? For whatever reasons, memories of his weeks with Michele homed in on him, weeks of unbroken sun with the Cassis harbor only faintly, and spottily, ruffled by breeze. Her skin had been darkly tanned and without contrasts, for her villa had been above the others on the face of the hill and she had sunbathed on its roof. Although Marseille was not so distant, her husband had come only on Friday and left on Sunday nights, and even during his stays she would sometimes manage an hour in Remington's room in the pension. *"Je ne peux plus le sentir,"* she had said of her husband. She had been twenty-three, married two years. "I can no longer smell him."

Remington could smell her now; something briny of salt and sweat, the scent of warmth—was there such a thing? And see the slack desiring look on her wide, unlipsticked mouth in the half-light filtering through the shutters of her villa's bedroom. And afterwards, the touch of a smile, her eyelids closed but fluttering sometimes, and her hair, brown with streaks of sunburned yellow, cast on the pillow around her head. And see her swimming slowly, spitting water through her lips. See her dining next to him at that outdoor restaurant, the whites of her eyes glistening in the dim light, digging the oysters from their shells and tipping the shells to her mouth to drink the juice. Tango music in the background.

Remington broke his reverie and walked to the window of his study. Darkness had fallen and across the court he could see kitchen maids at work on the evening meal. From his own kitchen he could hear the familiar coaxing of Jane being fed.

Then he had a thought which, for the moment, put the matter to rest. Unmarried or married, in the vicinity or not, if there was a single thing which he could say with certainty about Michele, it was that she had a lover. How long did he suppose she had remained without one after his departure from Cassis? A few days? A week at most. God knows he had connected with her quickly enough after their first meeting. *"Tu me plais terriblement, tu sais."* How many times she must have said that since!

But by the end of January he was thinking that, still and all, she had been mightily attracted to him, there had been no mistaking that. What difference would a current lover make except a complication in her schedule? At night, brushing his teeth, Remington sought out the changes of eight years in his mirrored image. The same short haircut above a more deeply lined, bonier forehead; a vein was visible in its middle which perhaps had not been evident then. How did she look now...?

Returning to the apartment in the evenings (he had not yet begun to write; there were still a few items to research) he began leaving the metro at the stop before Jasmin and sitting in a cafe near Rue de l'Assomption with an evening paper, hoping and suppressing the hope that she would walk through its door or see him there through the glass wall to the sidewalk. He told himself that he was there to avoid the irritating fuss of Jane's mealtime and Frankie's pale and, these days, increasingly tired face. He was sensibly waiting for Jane to be in bed and for Frankie to collect herself so that he would come home to a peaceful cocktail hour. But when he left the cafe his feet dragged.

He started writing toward the end of February which meant that he remained in the apartment all day. Between four and five in the afternoon he would go out for a walk, usually near Rue de l'Assomption, usually to the same news vendor, usually to the same cafe. He had passed Michele's building many times by now. He felt increasingly absurd.

If he were a man, and he really wanted to see this girl, why didn't he call her up? What was he doing, mooning around the neighborhood like an idiot adolescent? Well, he supposed there were reasons. If he called, it could only mean that he wanted her in bed, while if they met by "accident" perhaps their relationship could be put on another basis. But what other basis? He did want her in bed, it was only that he hesitated to introduce a disrupting element into his life. And what a stupid, in most ways unrewarding, element! He tried to remember Michele's conversation apart from the words of love. "Meet me at the cafe at seven...Tomorrow let's take a boat and picnic in the cove at the harbor's mouth." She had admired the songs of Yves Montand, he remembered. She had thought Marlon Brando an excellent actor. She had never been outside of France and had no wish to travel except to the Greek Islands. When he had asked why they attracted her more than other places she had replied that she didn't know. She was articulate to that degree. Who needed it?

She had asked him what he had been studying in Paris and when he had begun to talk about Bertrand de Born she had looked so startlingly vacuous that he had laughed. And he remembered her slightly husky voice speaking of inconsequential things, giving everything a monotonous, equal importance. Was she worth any effort at all?

Besides his work, the problem of Michele seemed to Remington quite enough for him to handle at this moment, but he realized there was another one for him to face. Frankie was fast losing her enthusiasm or had already lost it. When he proposed the theater one evening she said, "Oh, Rem, it's no use. My French simply isn't good enough for me to enjoy it." Wouldn't she go to Berlitz for intensive lessons? But when? He knew she was busy with Jane all day. The baby-sitter? But this opened a familiar argument. Frankie was determined to be Jane's nurse, no intermediaries allowed. But for a couple of hours during Jane's nap? Remington would get her up, if need be. "Oh," and she looked extremely tired, "what difference does it make? You go to the theater. You enjoy it." She had lost her palate for gourmet cooking. "Those sauces. They're making me dream of broiled steaks, or even tea and crackers." They were increasingly restricted to the apartment.

One cool, bright Sunday after lunch, Remington suggested that they call the sitter and go out by themselves for a walk on the left bank. Frankie was silent a moment, stirring her coffee, then said, "I think I'll take Jane to the *Bois*."

"It'll be crowded today. Leave her for a few hours. You don't have to obey your theory absolutely, Frankie."

"It's not a theory. It's what I want."

"Suit yourself." But he felt he must add. "You're pale, you know. I think it would do you good to get away from her once in a while."

"I suppose you think it would do her good, too."

"I didn't say that."

"You go walking," she said. "Have a good time."

When he had finished his coffee he went into the study, copied Michele's phone number on a scrap of paper and left the apartment without saying good-bye.

He left the metro at Rue de Bac and walked to the river. On the quai he deliberately slowed his pace, wanting to enjoy the Louvre in the sunlight ahead to his left, the flower vendor at the corner, and the antique shops on the Quai Voltaire. But his feet tramped faster, urged perhaps by the traffic straining for every possible bit of speed in the street beside him, until he crossed the Pont Neuf onto the comparatively quiet Ile de la Cite.

Why didn't he call Michele? An interview would at least set matters straight one way or the other. He would know either that they would have nothing to do with one another, because the attraction had gone or because she was somehow, or by someone, made incapable of arranging a rendezvous, or they would have an affair. And the latter possibility seemed much less dangerous now than it had at first. If he had not fallen in love with her seven years ago, there was no reason to suppose he would now. Ridding himself of this preoccupation would not only be a positive gain for his own life and work, Frankie might very well profit, too. Good humor and sympathy should come more easily to him than they did now. Very likely his being preoccupied had something to do with Frankie's depression.

Then why not? For a moment his brain was numb and the banks of the Seine and the people strolling and fishing there took on meaningful shapes, then the phrases of common wisdom began to occur to him. "The unity of the home once broken..." The destruction of complete confidence... The protection of the family, of Jane. Beneath these phrases was a fear, almost, absurdly, a certainty; it will show somehow. Then his mind went further back; "and cleave to her only...a sanctified estate..." That was where the "it will show" came from—the indelible mark of sin.

You sure as hell grew up in New England, Remington thought. You sure as hell went to Yale. And it was all a lot of nonsense.

If he made love (and why the genteel euphemism, for God's sake!) to Michele, it need neither be detected by Frankie nor subtly ruinous to their relationship. He could have spent an hour in Michele's apartment every afternoon for the last month without arousing the least suspicion.

A fifty franc piece, a telephone slug bought in any cafe, and he would know. Remington started walking slowly in the direction of Notre Dame. He saw a cafe down one of the cross streets and stopped and leaned against a wall, staring at it, then walked on.

He was a coward, that was the truth of it. Afraid to rock the boat. No matter how small the chance of detection, no matter that it might make him a pleasanter and more useful man, he didn't dare. Sheer cowardice. What came to the surface of his memory now was Michele's total sensuality. Swimming, he would touch her ankle or the luscious curve of her hip and they would stop and look at one another with faintly questioning little smiles. She would say, *"Ah, bon,"* and smile more broadly and they would swim to shore and grab their towels. They did not dry themselves, they let the sun do it climbing to her villa. And he remembered her nonchalant voice, "Let them talk. I don't give a damn what they think," full of the superiority of sensual satisfaction. She had it better than anyone, she was saying. Others would, of course, be jealous.

No. He could not afford that fading to inconsequence of the rest of the world. There was too much to lose.

He continued in the direction of Notre Dame, crossed the square in front of it, and entered the cathedral. After a look upwards at the glass he moved to one of the side chapels and knelt. The altar was nearly bare of objects, no candles burned, and the entire alcove looked dusty and forgotten. He had chosen an unpopular saint, he supposed. Lord, he thought, congratulate me on my cowardice. It has prevented me from being a better man, perhaps, but it has made me obey one of your commandments. What is your choice? Obedience or courage? Remington smiled as though he had scored a point in conversation, said aloud, "No answers here," and got up and went outside, smiling and feeling oddly settled.

That evening, from Frankie's quick, slightly fearful glances, Remington judged that she felt guilty for his abrupt departure. She filled the ice bucket for him and brought a bowl of peanuts into the living room which Jane passed between them again and again. He made the martinis, icing the glasses beforehand and shaving zests of lemon peel. It was a small celebration, of what, exactly, was uncertain. When they went to bed, Remington cupped her shoulder in his hand, feeling the frailness of her bones. Her forearm seemed as light and soft as a cat's paw. Later, postponing sleep for a few twilight moments, it seemed to him that the afternoon's decision had been unquestionably right. He would be insane to risk losing this sensitive and sympathetic Frankie whom he loved.

He did not entirely forget Michele, but her memory no longer disturbed his work. Nearly half the chapters were in draft now and he had not discovered any serious oversights in his research. The writings of French was coming easier after so long a layoff, and he began to foresee the manuscript's completion toward the end of June and the two whole free months of vacation, perhaps on the Riviera. His optimism affected Frankie, who, with the budding of the chestnut trees and the sky's change from wintry gray to milky blue, took color in her cheeks and a new, refreshing humor. Only in idle moments of subway riding or cafe sitting did Michele occur to him, and then she seemed a figure at fifty yards distance whom he could admire and at the same time patronize—a summer night's dream of long ago. With her image thus recessed from him, he could again consider his own with some complacency.

One morning near the end of July in the villa they had rented at Saint Jean Cap Ferrat he wrote FIN at the bottom of page 221, carefully aligned the pages, clipped them, and stacked the chapters in order in a stiff-sided carrying case that Frankie had given him especially for the purpose. He would not look at it again until they were on the boat, perhaps not until they were back in Wesleyan. He changed into his bathing suit, took flippers and mask from the closet, and walked down the rocks to the small pebbly beach. Jane, a lemony tan by now with a white duck hat strapped to her head, was shoveling pebbles into a small bucket and dumping them into the sea. Frankie, tanned and freckled at the same time, and covered overmodestly by the standards of this beach in a skirted suit, was stretched out near Jane on an air mattress. He crouched beside her and said, "Done!" and she jumped with surprise and then laughed.

"Martinis for lunch," he said, laughing too. "Do you want to swim?"

"I've just come out. Well," she said, staring at him. "Culture hero."

Sitting on a rock a few feet from shore Remington put on the flippers, wet the mask and bit the breathing tube, then pushed out into the clear water. He stayed close to shore looking for the smaller fish feeding near the surface. They were there, swishing their filmy tails while the legs of other swimmers flashed in the water above them. As Remington slowly kicked, the water rumbled like small, distant explosions in his ears, enclosing him. And the other swimmers were as removed by the medium of water as characters on a screen. How beautiful they were, the girls' shadowy undersides with the streaked sunlight reaching down one side and then the other as they rolled slightly, swimming. How beautiful the head-down, stretched-out pose of the fisherman, air gun aimed at a crevice in the rocks he was searching. How curiously restful, the bright ignoring fish.

Out and drying himself, he looked along the rocky cove at the sunbathers and at the people drinking and eating under the bright umbrellas on the hotel's terrace, and his perspective on the familiar scene seemed suddenly lengthened, and the world harmonized.

On the trip north to the ship at Le Havre he thought that the mood of their entire last month had been set by his swim after writing FIN. Was it the beginning of wisdom or the first signs of middle age? But he had continued to feel a peculiar isolation from the scene around him. His feelings toward it were benign—indeed, he and Frankie seemed contented together as never before. He no longer sensed strain in her, and their silences were at ease. A glance, and "I'll get it." Remington thought that from his new point of vantage he might produce more happiness for Frankie and Jane than when he was closer to them, more nakedly emotional and selfish. Perhaps a sober and important lesson had been learned: that life was best managed and appreciated by the underwater swimmer to whom the shapes and details and movements around him are absolutely clear and yet who keeps his hands clear and is not touched.

■　　■　　■

Not third class, as on his first transatlantic voyage, not first class yet (and maybe never), but second class, and the cabin seemed comfortable enough, and the steward friendly.

The evening of their first full day on board they sat up late in the bar talking with a couple who had spent a year much like their own. He was an instructor at Chicago and had had a Fulbright at Grenoble. Stendhal, of course, and his wife, oddly, had been in training as a nursery-school teacher. She was a sort of girl Frankie was suspicious of, overserious and fiercely academic, but Remington liked the man and thought they would be at least passable company during the four days ahead. The familiar, but long absent, bookish talk invigorated him and made him nervous, reminding him of all he had not read during the year.

The Chicago man had apparently been totally unaffected by Europe. He looked and talked as though he had just stepped out of a classroom and was ready instantly to enter another and begin his lecture. Beside him, Remington felt juicy with southern sun, good wine, and garlic, his brain blunted by the lazy rhythm of the life they had been leading. When he and Frankie reached their cabin he got out a bottle of cognac and poured himself a dollop in the toothbrush glass. "How did you like them?" he asked softly. Jane was asleep on the opposite side of the cabin from their bunks.

"A breath of stale air," she said. She was fumbling with the zipper at her back and Remington reached up and pulled it.

"Nothing seems to have happened to them in Europe," he said. "I wonder if they thought the same of us."

Frankie glanced at him, stepping out of her dress. "We have better sunburns. Bigger freckles."

"And a Citroen car, and we're all one year older. Come on, Frankie."

She crossed her arms over her slip. "Things have happened," she said. "I went through something last winter..."

"I didn't realize."

"I thought you had," she said. She pulled her slip over her head, shivered, and put on her bathrobe. "I thought there was something on your mind, too."

As he restrained himself from admitting to it, he thought, now I'm twice a coward. "The thesis bogged down there, for a while." He poured more brandy and when he looked up, saw a glint of childlike suspicion in Frankie's eyes. Why had she the power to make him cowardly? Of all people, Frankie, to whom he had lent his strength so often? "What was bothering you?" he asked.

She mimicked, "The thesis bogged down there, for a while."

He sat down on the bunk and gazed at the floor.

"I thought I was losing you," she said.

"Well, you weren't. Just the opposite."

"There was something, then."

"Nothing."

"Just that bogging thesis."

"Let's forget about it, Frankie. Let's go to bed." But when he reached for her hand, she drew it away.

"You'd better tell me."

Why not tell her if she was so anxious to hear it? The story, was all to his credit as a husband.

"All right," he said, "you'll see. Eight years ago I knew a girl in the south of France—"

"I remember."

"She wrote me a couple of letters after I'd come home, and in the last one, she told me she'd divorced her husband—"

"Convenient."

"—and had moved to Paris. I'd forgotten all about her until one day in the flat I found her in an old address book. She lived just a couple of streets away from us." Remington paused but Frankie said nothing. "I never laid eyes on her, Frankie."

"Was that your trouble?"

"I would have liked to have seen her. I would have liked to introduce you, as a matter of fact. But I decided that nothing was worth the chance of upsetting you or our marriage. So I never spoke to her or saw her. That's the whole story."

"Just nothing at all. It was just enough to keep you incommunicado for about three months."

"If I wasn't saying much, don't blame her. The thesis wasn't going very well, and that's the truth."

"Three months of silence on account of some little tart you knew eight years ago? That's some marriage."

"You're upset over nothing, Frankie."

"I'll tell you what's nothing..." She moved to the end of the bunk where he could not see her face. He leaned forward and saw that she was crying.

"Frankie."

"Don't 'Frankie' me. Three months as a housekeeper because you're mooning over a French tart. A 'Frankie' used to fix that, I guess. And when your mind is free at last, you're kind to me, like in Saint Jean. That isn't good enough any more, either. You've never loved me, Remington. You never would have married me if I hadn't told you I had an income. It never crossed your mind before I told you that. With twenty thousand dollars thrown in you could afford to be nice to Frankie."

Remington stood up. "Any other crazy ideas?"

"Plenty." She was clinging to the bunk's stanchion. "Do you know why I'm not pregnant? Because I didn't want to be. I didn't want to be if you were thinking of somebody else when you made love to me. You have no idea what it's like."

"Well, that *is* crazy. You didn't even know another girl existed until right now."

"But I felt something and I didn't want your child until I knew what it was. Now I know and I still don't want to be pregnant."

Remington began to walk the floor, without much dignity due to the rolling of the ship. "I've never seen you like this, never thought I would."

"I've grown up. I don't want your handouts any more. I don't want to be in misery for six months because you're having a selfish little quarrel with yourself about whether or not you're going to see a French tart. You can go to hell."

"The bar is where I'm going. I won't listen anymore."

She remained silent while he straightened his tie and put on his jacket. When he was at the door she said, "I hope my money buys good scotch."

The lounge was empty except for one engrossed couple. The bartender, polishing what were presumably the evenings last glasses, didn't look happy to see him. "Are you closing?" Remington asked.

"I hope so."

"Give me a double scotch and I won't keep you."

When Remington had it he chose a chair as far as possible from the couple and sat staring aft at the gray, thrashing wake—all that was visible in the overcast night.

If only he had followed his impulse and had had an affair with Michele! He wouldn't have been "incommunicado." Indeed, guilty, he would have been sweeter and more attentive to Frankie than before. If she had sensed some mystery in his life, too, it would have added to his power. And now instead...he had not eaten his cake and did not have it, and what was infinitely more serious, they were not at the end of something, but only at the beginning. For if Frankie believed what she had said, and that these attitudes were "grown up" it could only mean that her thoughts had been moving in this direction for some time. And to reverse them...?

Remington could hear the campus gossip and see Frankie, erratic on her own, doing wild things to hurt him—mocking him to his colleagues, undercutting him. She might even have an affair with someone, maybe even an undergraduate. If *only* he had had his affair with Michele!

He sipped his drink, anger making his breath short, and looked around at the nuzzling couple. That vacant look of passion. Why the hell didn't they go to bed?

He turned back to the tumbling wake and sipped again, wrenching his mind to Wesleyan and Hartford. Out of the well of possible disasters came a face, Betty Law's, and he considered its blue eyes and funnily pouting mouth. As far as he knew she was still unmarried, still working for Equitable. And another face, Dee Vanderle's. Divorced now from the man who had succeeded Remington as her lover and living in New York.

Yes, New York, thought Remington, and we will be there one whole week before going up to Wesleyan.

LIFE AFTER BOOZE

"Booze," Arthur said, like a headline. "Is there life after booze?"

"I'm alive," Mitchell answered. But he sounded dead to his own ears. Had he ever felt at ease in this crowd, sober?

"You're telling me, yes," Arthur went on, "but how you can stand this party without drinking, I don't know. Celebrate Gretchen's 'debut' *dry*?"

Women in pink and white were standing in the summer living room's open barn doors, their dresses tinted orange by the setting sun. One of them was shading her eyes to look down at two men in blue blazers sitting on the floor, in shadow, and Mitchell saw that it was Dorothy, in the lotus position with her back against a sofa, who had drawn them.

"I see where you're looking, old chum. What a pair you were, lucky bastard! Now you're a new person, does my saying that bother you? A great girl, she is. Do you know that?"

"I knew that, Arthur."

"You use the past tense. Now you're a clean and upright fellow, maybe you don't think so?"

Mitchell watched Dorothy lean forward for a light, saw her glance at him in its flare, and then her familiar jet of whistled-out smoke. He said, distractedly, "You must have seen that I was falling apart, back then."

"Are you saying she was responsible for that?" There were chalky pouches under Arthur's eyes, suddenly, for his face had turned pink. "It wasn't Dorothy that made a mess of you, Mitchell. You'd have to look elsewhere for the cause."

"Myself. No doubt of it." Indeed, when he had connected with Dorothy his job had already been in jeopardy. His wife had left him months before, thanking God that they'd had no children. His driver's license had been suspended, and he was heavily in debt to his father.

It had sometimes seemed funny to Mitchell that these disasters in his life had been accompanied by an elevation of his social status. Before his divorce, and Dorothy, he had been unknown to this evening's guests. But the new invitations had more often seemed to him, in his boozy egotism, solemn evidence that his wife had undervalued him and held him back.

Arthur was puffed up, and continuing. "I'd say that you were looking at someone who was loyal to you if you'd given her the chance, and who, in my opinion, got damned little benefit from your attentions."

"No argument."

"No argument," Arthur was repeating scornfully when Gretchen tugged Mitchell's elbow, and hard.

"Hello! Hello, Mitchell! There's someone I want you to meet. Excuse us, Arthur."

Mitchell followed her through the noisy crowd, keeping his eyes on her upswept hair, blonder than it used to be, and held by a tortoiseshell comb. Outside the barn doors, she turned and said, "There isn't anyone to meet, I hope you don't mind. Your conversation with Arthur just looked awfully sticky."

"I'm grateful. I wasn't prepared for it."

"Then I'm glad I rescued you." Gretchen's smile was new and shining, striking, because two years ago she had worn black-rimmed glasses and had seemed continually pale-faced and sore around the nostrils from allergies. Now her yellowish brown eyes were large and clear—behind contact lenses, he supposed.

He had known her for years, without knowing her. Her Boy Scoutish ex-husband, Dan, had worked with him in the same department at the Sub Yard and had clearly disapproved of Mitchell's drinking, never would have asked him to a cup of coffee. Then, at a moment when Mitchell's troubles had seemed to him the world's only troubles, Dan had vanished with one of Gretchen's occasional baby-sitters to start a new life in Puerto Rico.

Gretchen looked back into the room. "Arthur might follow you, he's so jealous."

"Just the notion of that..."

"Not about me, of course," she said quickly, "about Dorothy. Didn't you know? And he has a drinking problem—you don't mind my saying that, I hope."

Two couples came up to thank Gretchen and say good night, nodding only faintly to Mitchell. When they'd left she said, "They'll all start to leave now. I hope you won't. I'm going to say no to invitations out to dinner, and since you aren't drinking I'd hoped—oh, help." Another departing couple had arrived and Mitchell stepped aside.

The sun had gone down, and the sky over Webster Point was magenta-streaked and darker purple. Old stone walls made fuzzy lines across the fields, and nearer, on the narrow strip of bay water, lay the fleet of bare-boomed dinghies in which children learned to sail. The party barked and trilled behind him.

Gretchen touched his arm and said, "I thought you might like to have something to eat here with me, rather than with a lot of drinking people."

"I really would."

Her smile shone. "Well! That wasn't so hard!"

At Gretchen's direction, he walked from the converted barn to her house, a nineteenth century monster which had always looked out of place to him in the borough. She had it for sale, he knew, but who would want it?

Attached to the kitchen door was a little rubber ball that swung out and cushioned the slam if the door were let go, and inside was a kitchen that might have been his boyhood's on the far side of town, except that it was brightly painted and equipped with new gadgetry. There were breakfronts along one wall, and a big, zinc-covered table. In his parents' house, his father's coveralls would have been hanging over the corner wash-sink, dripping. This one had been covered over, and a wine rack stood on it.

He had come home partly to make what amends he could to his parents, and that morning he had had coffee with them in their retirement apartment back of Mystic. He had set forth his plan to settle his debt, but had not been happy with how it had gone. His father's skepticism was understandable, but it had been hard to sit across from his sad eyes and tough little smile. His mother had acted as she had years ago when his father's boss and his wife had come to dinner, that mixture of affection and fear. His father had worked for the same man for thirty years, but early in that span when the Depression had hit hardest he had laid his father off for six months.

His mother had served a coffee cake that she knew Mitchell liked, but he had had difficulty eating it, feeling that her buying it had defied his father.

Now Mitchell sat down and ran his fingers on the cool, nubbly zinc, hearing a man's voice calling outside, "Peter! Sue! Time's come, everybody."

The door spring twanged, and Dorothy walked in and let the door bounce behind her. "Mitchell." Full stop. "Hidden away over here? Why should Mitchell, a hero to us all, someone who faced his problem squarely and dealt with it, why should Mitchell be tucked out of sight in the kitchen?" She came toward him with a dark highball in hand. "How are you, sweetie? Big kiss." When he did not rise to kiss her she said, "Doesn't want a big kiss? Because it smells of booze?"

"Sit down, Dorothy."

Her glass thumped on the zinc, spilling a bit. "What would be of interest to you, laudable Mitch? News of bankruptcies? Of cruises which ended love affairs and friendships?"

"You have a nice intuition, Dorothy."

She said, "I'm sorry I couldn't write you a letter. There was too much or too little in me, your superficial friend. You look well— don't tell me I do. But you weren't going to, were you?" She sipped.

"Did you really have to go to that awful place? You could have kept your job, I know that."

"I just could not stop drinking, Dorothy. You only saw a fraction."

"You looked like Norman Normal to me, all the Normals around here being soused a lot."

"I'm glad to hear I looked like Norman."

"You should be." They laughed together. "Hell," she said, "are you really all right? Really and truly? I think maybe your soul has gone into a deep freeze."

"No."

"Ah, but maybe. I suppose you had to get sober, but maybe you pay a price for it."

"It doesn't feel like a price," he said. "It feels like a payoff."

She looked sad and then warm and lustful for a moment. "Behind your noble, Chippendale facade beats a heart of vinyl formica, perhaps."

"It's a big change, no booze, but I don't think anything has atrophied."

"You pompous jerk." She got out a cigarette and waited for a light. Her eyes were teary. "Are you here for the night? Longer?"

"Tonight and tomorrow."

"Call me. No you won't, will you?"

"I won't. It's not easy for me, Dorothy."

"Prig," she said. "Coward."

Mitchell stood up and turned the gas up under the kettle. Dorothy's chair scraped and then she went to the door and opened it. "Bye," she said. The door closed, then reopened. "I'm going to answer your letter. It's just come to me, pages of it, and the foolscap I'll write it on. Give me your address."

He looked for a note pad but then remembered that he had a business card.

"Service manager," she read. "Isn't that sweet? How many trucks?"

"Five," he said, although there were in fact nearly forty.

"That makes me forget my letter, foolscap notwithstanding."

A man's voice—Arthur's voice—called, "Dorothy?" not far outside the screen door, but beyond the range of light. She continued staring at the card. "Dorothy?" he called again.

Mitchell said, "Stop it, now, and go along."

"Hey! Dorothy."

She put the card down on the table. "I don't think I can write a service manager. An alcoholic, yes. Someone down-and-out, yes. A service manager, I don't think so. Laugh, you son of a bitch."

"Dorothy, go along now."

"But, of course. You're waiting for your new, myopic and witty admirer, aren't you? She's hidden you away here for safekeeping, as well she might. Knows her engineers, that woman. If you haven't already, I'm not sure I'd go into it about service manager."

Mitchell went to the door and held it open. As she passed him she breathed bourbon saying, "Frigid, her husband used to tell me. You'll confirm or deny, of course."

Mitchell poured out Dorothy's drink and sat down with a cup of instant coffee that looked extremely hot. There was a creaking noise in his temples, a noise that used to send him straight to the bar. He got up and paced the kitchen, then escaped it, going outside into the dark, away from both buildings. After some walking he sat down against a tree.

When the last car had driven off, Mitchell met Gretchen on her way to the kitchen, startling her. "I thought you'd gone. Someone said there was no one."

"Let me help you clean up."

She protested, but he knew it would help him to work at something. They were quick about it, carrying in the glasses and platters and stacking them in the washer.

"Record time!" she said. She took a pot of stew from the refrigerator, put it in the wall oven to warm, and went about making a salad. "You won't mind if I have a glass of wine?"

"Oh, no. I like this room," he said, and compared it to his childhood kitchen.

"I've loved this house," she said, "but it's for sale and I don't want to love it too much."

"Are your children upset?"

"They've got to adjust because I've got to sell it. That sounds tough, I suppose."

"But it's wise not to carry pains you can't do anything about. Some of those are on my mind."

"They couldn't not be. All these old sights to you."

"I met with my parents this morning," he said. "I can do something for them, if I stick with it, but there are other situations there's nothing to be done about, and I'd better not brood on them."

After a moment she said, "I had a hard day, too."

"Yes? You didn't show it."

"I'm glad of that. If that's true, I'm glad as can be. Now I can go away if I want, and I think I want to. I felt I had to have a party, alone, a summer cocktail party with people in their nice clothes. The new me."

"You did it, and it was just right."

"Seems silly to you, probably, silly and conventional, but you see, Dan brought me here. It's his town, or was. And I came and made babies and felt like hell most of the time. Then he left me. That puts a mark on a girl."

"No marks," Mitchell said. "No marks at all. You're much prettier."

"So?" She giggled. It was a disused sound, and touching. "Honest to Pete? I wasn't at all pretty as a kid, or in high school. Then in college where I met Dan, I was, some. At least I thought so. But when the children were young I really couldn't bear to look at myself, I felt so plain. I hated myself. If I've made a comeback, I'm so pleased!"

"It was just a question of finding the right disasters, for both of us."

"And the right allergy pills," she said, "and contact lenses."

"The correct reduction in income."

"And not caring what the kids think. Tell me," she said. "Will you help me leave these dishes? Not touch them at all?" Then she seemed uncomfortable. "I don't want to be cute, or flip. I don't know how to be, or what to be. That's the truth."

"I feel a lot the same."

"You're lonely," she said. "All your old ties are gone or confused, and no new ones. I see that."

"You're right."

"I'm so happy right now," she said. "I hope you're happy."

"I am."

She laughed and reached across the table for his hand. "I'm very happy, us sitting here. I thought I might never be able to do this. Mummy could, but she was so pretty."

Gretchen lay asleep with the ruffles of her nightgown around her chin. Mitchell's eyes were wide.

He got up carefully and crossed the bedroom to sit at a moonlit window. From it he could see the west side of the town going out to the silhouette of the old lighthouse, never in service in his lifetime, and the red and green flashing lights on the breakwaters. The town looked small and was small, of course, just as he had known it to be as a child. Then when it had given him "best boy" awards, a Lion's Club scholarship, and a starting job better paid than his father's, it had swollen, together with his ego. When he'd been arrested, drunk and disorderly (Dennis the cop, his old friend, ripping his shirt!), when he'd been delinquent on everything, pretending to himself he was still fair-haired and rising, the town had seemed enormous. It had become even larger as the judge, with Mitchell's parents and a doctor in the courtroom, had said that he'd grant probation on felony drunk driving only on condition Mitchell would enter a recovery program.

Gretchen moved, then sat up suddenly. "Why are you there? You should be here, not over there."

"I woke up and couldn't sleep. Too happy."

She sank back and, after a moment, said softly, "Does happiness make you uneasy? Sometimes I think it does me."

He slipped in beside her. "I don't think, before, I ever was truly happy."

"You'll be happy," she said, dreamily. "That's what you set out to be and you will be, because you're strong."

"Not strong, Gretchen."

"Oh, yes. You were strong enough to get everything you thought you wanted, and now you're strong enough to quit the bottle. Doing that is very strong! I never had the guts to risk the big addictions, and I've still got all my little ones. Chiclets."

"When you hit bottom, Gretchen, strength doesn't help. Instead, you have to give up, let go."

"But that's magical! While my Chiclets—lists, three cups of coffee in the morning—are just dreary. I guess I'm jealous of your misfortunes and how you've coped with them."

"You've made much too nice a picture of me, Gretchen."

"Maybe," she said. "But I've got to believe there are larger things in life than Chiclets." Her voice deepened. "It can't hurt that I admire you, can it? I've lived in such dread of little things, and here you've walked back into your hometown with your head up. You're even in bed with the hostess, for God's sake!" They laughed together, and he put his arms around her. Snuggling her head into his shoulder she said, "Let me admire you a bit. Let me be happy." This time, though, her warmth was soon too warm, and her head became heavy on his shoulder.

Mitchell woke at five, breathless and rigid. Admired.

He quietly picked up his clothes and carried them downstairs, dressed, and left the house. He drove to Water Street and stopped a minute opposite the old stores—news and candy, antiques, real estate. Their windows were dusty and blank in the early light. Then he continued on to the tiny square, War of 1812 cannons on the triangle of grass, and back on Main, past the town's best houses. None of it affected him.

He drove over the railroad bridge toward Westerly and as the familiar landmarks passed he foresaw every side road or drive he could turn around in, but he did not use them.

He parked about fifty yards up the street from Al's Schooner, open six AM. At twelve to six none of the early birds were around, an important point. An arrival at six oh two convinced them that they could take the stuff or leave it alone.

Al drove up to the side of his place and Mitchell heard him unlocking in back, then in front.

Jack was the first to appear, dressed spic-and-span for business, as always. Mitchell thought he must take a belt at home to get him through his dressing. Two men Mitchell didn't know went in and then a woman, a boutique sort of woman.

Ray found him. Mitchell had forgotten that Ray habitually parked in a side street and would pass his car.

"Well, look here," Ray said. "How long's it been?" He was chewing Dentyne or something like it, and its smell mingled, but did not mix, with the smell of stale whiskey.

"A couple of years."

"You ain't been drinking a couple of years?"

"That's right."

Ray stepped back blinking and looking suspicious. "I ain't buying," he said.

"I'm not asking."

"What are you doing here, then?"

Mitchell shook his head.

"You come here so we'll tell you you're a good boy, congratulations?"

"No."

"If I was you, you come here to show off, I'd get a shave, put a necktie on, bring along your bank statement." Ray said, "Get out of here, Mitch. Beat it."

Ray walked toward the bar with his hands jammed in his windbreaker pockets and his feet hitting the sidewalk unevenly. Mitchell could feel the tenderness in Ray's heels and the balls of his feet, and knew he'd be doing an aerial act until he could get outside a couple. Seagram's Seven was his drink, Seven with a side of water. Mitchell's stomach gripped itself with envy.

From a phone booth in Westerly, Mitchell called the AA number, waking an old man who had trouble hearing. He hung up and drove on to New London and down to the waterfront. He walked a long time, studying the improvements being made to the port, making blueprints of them in his mind, and staring across the water at the Groton Sub Yard. The morning grew hot and the haze thickened.

He knocked at Gretchen's door around ten, and she came to open it wearing the old black-rimmed glasses, a bandana around her hair, T-shirt, and jeans. "Good morning," she said. "Like a cup of coffee?"

He thanked her and said he would. "I've got to talk, mainly, Gretchen. I want to tell you some things that I want you to understand. I've got to tell you where I went this morning. Why, also."

"You certainly do, it seems." She went to the stove, leaned down to light the burner, and when she looked up her expression was fragile.

Mitchell said, "Maybe you're way ahead of me."

"Oh, I don't think so. Not me, brother." She said, "Won't you sit down? I'm nervous. You don't have to say it all at once, surely."

"True." They sat at opposite ends of the table and Mitchell said, "Truth to tell, I don't know where to begin. I haven't started and I'm tired out already."

"Let's just start anywhere," she said. "I don't have to admire you. You don't have to like me, or explain anything."

"I like you for saying that."

"And I've got a real estate agent arriving with a prospect in about two minutes, and I feel like a harridan."

"I could show them around, Gretchen. I can even show them how they built these houses. No expense spared on foundations, plumbing, or wiring!"

"Where did you go, Mitch? You haven't been drinking, have you?"

"No. The first drink wasn't far off, but, no. Ah, that worry hasn't helped you much, has it?"

"If you'd gone to get drunk," she said, "it might have helped me, in a way. It would have been a reason for you to disappear like that. If you weren't getting drunk, you see, you'd just up and left. I'd been left again."

He said, "I never for a second thought of that, I'm that stupid. I'm a stupid egomaniac."

She drummed her nails on the table, then said, "I think I just told you that I'd have preferred that you drink yourself to death rather than take a walk on me. Does that sound at all egomaniacal to you?"

"That's just terrible," he said.

"Not as bad as you."

"You're right."

"No," she said. "I'm worse." She threw her head back and laughed.

"Shall I call the police and turn us both in?"

"Listen," she said, "we can fight about it later. There's a razor of Dan's in the downstairs john. Chiclet—frugal.

I couldn't throw it out." She hurried upstairs, and Mitchell went to shave.

Gretchen showed the house to a wary couple, dressed for church. Then she and Mitchell made a picnic and took it to the beach.

Her bikini probably dated to her "pretty" days in college, for it seemed unlike her now, not that her body didn't look lovely in it. When she walked down to the water or along the sand collecting shells, every stride and gesture gave him a pleasure he'd forgotten.

At the afternoon's end, Mitchell had to start the long drive to Schenectady. They stood inside her front door at formal distance from one another.

"Thank you," he said.

"Thank you."

"I like you a lot."

"If you say anything more than that," she said, "it could be the end of everything."

"You, too," he replied. "No extreme statements!"

"Whatever made you think I'd make one?"

He groaned, and they laughed.

"Your nose is going to peel," she said. "Do you want a thermos of something?"

"I can't think of what. Don't you ever burn?"

"I burn."

When they hugged she said, "I'm afraid I'll hurt you."

"You won't," he said. "Will you?"

"No. You wouldn't me?"

"Oh, no."

His car was baking hot, and he felt the sweat starting in his pores. The landmarks, as he drove the back roads to the thruway, were vivid and painful. In the bright, late sunshine the leaves of every passing tree were distinct, many shades of green.

Later, in the twilight and then the dark, his senses turned inward to snatches of fantasy, luxuriant scenes through which Gretchen floated, smiling. Happy endings. Bringing his senses back to the highway he felt his stomach clenched, and knew that that was what he must not do. Do not believe in the merry-go-round's brass rings. She must not, either. Stay in memory, *genuine* memory, her voice saying, "That wasn't so hard." Stay on the dry, firm highway, and live to see what might happen, one day at a time.

A NEW OCEAN

At five in the afternoon one day in the fall of 1963 my "guide" took the sleep mask from my eyes and helped me to sit up on the deep couch on which I'd been lying since eight that morning. He told me that the mixture of LSD and mescaline that I'd been given had now passed through my system. How did I feel?

I could not answer him. The drugs had tilted my brain and breached a barrier, and visions from my subconscious had been pouring unstoppably into my conscious mind. Some had been literal, or had made me laugh—the desk I'd worked at in the Ivory Coast, a snapshot of a friend's expanded waistline—but most had been so heavy with significance and reproach that they had squeezed my heart to groaning. My father's wide eyes and yearning, boyish smile, shadowed by the brim of his fedora, had fixed me. At his death several years before, our difficulties had been unresolved. A Chanel suit belonging to my separated wife hung flatly in a dim and empty closet. My four-year-old daughter's thin legs and pretty shoes had skipped back and forth, back and forth. My hair behind the temples, and the cushion that had been under my head, were soaked with tears.

My guide led me to a chair before a window and drew its curtain wide. "How does it look to you?"

"Awful." An asphalt parking lot stretched to a tree-lined street down which cars appeared to be moving at violent speed. Solitary people were squinting against the slanted autumn sunshine.

"Do you want to go out there?"

"No, I don't."

He wrapped a blanket around me, for I was shivering, and left the room. Beyond the closed door I heard the murmur of a consultation, and I could picture him with the blond woman doctor who had checked me physically and had replaced him at my side when he needed relief, and with the wiry psychoanalyst who was the program's director. There were others of the staff, but I could not identify the voices.

Some of these others had medical or therapeutic credentials, some did not, but titles and qualifications seemed unimportant to them. They were of all ages and complexions. Something they believed could change the world had been discovered, and anyone of useful intelligence would probably have been welcomed by them. Not long before, John Kennedy had spoken about Space as "the new ocean," saying that we must sail on it simply for that reason, because it was a new ocean, and this group shared that spirit. So far, they had every reason to be optimistic about these inner-space voyages.

The friend of mine who had proposed insistently that I take the drugs, who knew the extent of my depression since my separation from wife and child nearly a year before, had worn a most unexpected, beatific smile from the day of his session onward, and he was not exceptional. The short-term benefits to troubled lives had been excellent, and no one had broken down.

My guide came back into the room and said, "We're going to give you something more. OK?" He was pale, and his dark stubble looked days old.

"Good."

A vertical cannister of CO_2 was wheeled in and a breathing mask attached over my face. A valve was turned, and the sound of rushing air filled my mind. I breathed deeply and was suddenly weightless and flying, relieved of my body. Without friction, without any sense of speed, I shot straight up into the constellations, and there, in the star-dotted blackness, I arrived at peace. My heart was freed, and in a silence in which there was no temperature, no gravity, no wish or will or conflict, no need, I felt an overwhelming, blissful gratitude.

I rested there a while and then I started down. The earth was far away, a speck and then a dime against the blackness, but it quickly grew. The continents and the oceans became distinct, the tan deserts, the ice at the poles, and the dark forests of Canada, Russia, and Africa. I began to see the conglomerations of towns and cities, and to sense the variety of people, especially those where I'd lived—in New York, in Paris, in Abidjan, and San Francisco. Nearing the ground I recognized with starts of joy some faces in the crowds, and I saw with the force of revelation that my father and my wife, and others whose specters had distressed me, were the same size as the rest, as robust and as frail.

As I slipped into my body and the floor became real under my feet, I felt my essential sameness with all these thousands of beings around me who were speaking in hundreds of tongues. Their warmth invaded me, and when I opened my eyes I was shouting with excitement at joining the world of humans.

My guide greeted my arrival and others came into the room to pat my back. After a time, one of them took me out into an evening of commonplace miracles.

I watched the ash-yellow oatfields rippling in a windless sunset, and found that I could see the sap moving in the branches of the live oak trees, even in the capillaries of the leaves. After dark, the lighted bridges crossing San Francisco Bay were bemusing, as were those wonders of human order, traffic lights. In many of the people we encountered I saw beauty of body or spirit, and every one of them seemed a miracle of gathered energy. Now so would I be.

My friend of the beatific smile had talked about "psychoanalysis in a day," but this was something much better, I thought. There was no need for "analysis." I was free.

■   ■   ■

Next morning I learned from a waitress at the counter of a strangely quiet, twenty-four-hour-a-day restaurant that John Kennedy had been shot in Dallas. He had been taken to a hospital. That was what was known.

I had never seen such things as the scrambled eggs on the faintly patterned, brownish plate, or the nicks in the tines of the fork. Yet I ate. My mind attempted sporadically to interpret the news, and at other moments, images from the day before took over. A man standing beside me spoke up in a loud voice, proposing a date to the waitress, and she turned pink and hurried away to the kitchen. The episode seemed no stranger than the food or the coffee.

The follow-up appointment with my guide was for eleven o'clock, still an hour away. I started walking without purpose and stopped outside a barbershop, for in it I could see a TV set turned on.

Both of the barbers were idle, one sitting in his chair, the other leaning against the back of his. Closest to the set was a black shoe-shine man, an older man, sitting. Their concentration was such that I momentarily felt I should not disturb them, but I went in and was motioned to sit down.

The TV camera was at the hospital. Just after the barber had begun to snip my hair the announcement came that Kennedy had died.

The shine man pointed at my shoes, but I shook my head. He said, "They couldn't let him live. Not after Bay of Pigs. Couldn't let him live his *life.*"

The broadcast went back in time to Kennedy's arrival at the Dallas airport with Jackie. Smiling officials greeted them. He was handsome and jaunty. Everyone was full of daylight.

"See him there?" the shine man said. "He's too much for them. Too much. They can't abide it."

The broadcast showed pictures of the motorcade, of the cars coming into Dealey Plaza. Then it was broken into and a voice told us that a suspect had been arrested, and that his name was Lee Harvey Oswald.

"They get someone. Oh, yes."

The images shifted to the hospital again, to Washington about the governmental consequences.

The shine man said, "He let them look real bad. CIA. Military, too." He wiped his eyes with his knuckle. "*Lee Harvey Oswald,* indeed."

I paid the barber and walked to my appointment.

My guide had not yet come in and when he did, brisk and clean shaven, he seemed too glad to see me. We sat at his desk and he asked some clinical questions. Had I slept? Had I dreamed? Was I experiencing flashbacks?

Then he dropped that manner. "Are you really OK? I thought of you first thing after I took in the shock, whether or not you'd be all right."

"I'm OK."

"I was afraid you might lose it, the good stuff you finally got yesterday."

"I've got it still," I told him.

"You were tough," he said. "You wouldn't let go. I tried what I could to help you though... Then the news. It's your universe. And then." His face showed pain, but a more superficial frustration as well. His treatment had been interfered with. He said, "Maybe you'll want to take it again. Do some more exploring."

I was embarrassed to be talking about myself, my case. "Not tomorrow," I said.

"Oh, no. Maybe months from now, certainly not tomorrow."

It was a strange handshake. The muscles of his hand and his skin were extraordinarily vivid, although there was nothing unusual about them.

I spent most of the next few days alone in my San Francisco apartment, the TV showing me the aftermath, the official events, the caisson crossing the Potomac Bridge. Sometimes I felt I knew where he had gone, out there in the cosmos. I could feel its weightless silence. For me it had been paradisiacal, but for him the timing was all wrong.

My apartment off Buena Vista Park had a small balcony which looked out on a sweep of the city's south side that included Twin Peaks, Diamond and Dolores Heights, and the bay toward San Leandro. Some of the Victorian houses facing me had been whimsically trimmed with bright paint. Wind chimes and bicycles hung on back stairway landings. I brooded on these clues to their inhabitants, and on the backyard gardens below me, some neatly planted, others beaten down around a children's swing, a kiln, a trampoline. Mad and dangerous though some of my neighbors no doubt were, I admired their putting the next meal on the table, doing what they had to, and getting on with it. I was of them as I had not been before.

Fifteen years afterwards I decided to find out what I could about the people who had run the program and those who had passed through it. I knew it had been shut down when LSD had been declared an illegal drug not long after my session.

I called the woman doctor who had sat with me part of the day. She had become a psychiatrist with a practice in Menlo Park.

On the phone she sounded professional and guarded, but said she would be glad to talk. I asked her if she'd like to meet for lunch, or any other time that suited, but she said, "You can make an appointment, if you like. I'll have to charge my fee." I was mildly shocked, but accepted her terms.

Her office was near where the Center had been, and it seemed a standard therapist's environment with comfortable dark chairs and a couch, and the curtains half-drawn. She was very much as I remembered her, a blond woman, somewhat overweight, with a smile that at moments looked tentative, at others a touch cynical.

She told me that when they had had to stop the program there had been no money to follow up on those like me. She could not tell me anything about long-term results, except in isolated cases. "Now you'll be one," she said. "What's happened to you?"

I told her that I'd remarried and had two younger children, and that I'd continued to teach and write. I'd published a novel and shorter pieces, and with another writer I'd started an annual writers' conference. On the other hand, that I felt I hadn't been productive enough. I had had a drinking problem but I had quit five or six years before. "What about you?" I asked.

"You can see," she said, without much enthusiasm. She added wryly, "I still haven't lost weight."

There was not much news she could give me of the others who had been on the staff. So-and-so was still working at Syntex, another had taken a job in Los Angeles. In her responses there was a shade of tedium, but also sympathy.

I asked about the psychoanalyst-director.

"He's at a Vets Administration hospital in Maryland. I have the feeling that he's serving out his time."

Did she remember that Kennedy had been killed the day after my session?

"Oh, yes. Yes. That day changed a lot of things for us. For everyone."

"What changed?"

"You know as well as I do. Many things."

"Things always change."

Her mouth twitched impatiently, but she replied, "The mood. The feeling of the possible."

We said good-bye and wished each other luck.

Outside the building's sunny entrance I stopped to look at a live oak tree, an old one with a great reach of gnarled branches and glistening dark leaves, which stood protected in the middle of a traffic island. I concentrated on it and, after a bit, I saw the sap moving in its newer, lighter limbs. The vision soon vanished and I could not revive it, although I was patient, blinking and staring intensely.

Then I let the effort go. Rather, it was swept aside by a rush of gratitude, part warm from memory, part fresh. A buoyant wave that lifted me from what had seemed a flat sea.

SOME RICH MILES

The Indian said, "One of the hard things for me, they say you got to love the other people in the Program. See, I grew up hating you people, white people." Some thirty of us, sober alcoholics like himself were sitting in the basement room, possibly once the ballroom, of a grand Victorian house.

"I get to say that here to you. I guess that's good. I hate my foreman. He'd be a son of a bitch black, green, or ivory—I think so. But maybe, you know, he's white. Anyways I haven't taken that first drink in a while. I'm doing it one day at a time." He grunted and got some sympathetic laughter.

Two others spoke briefly and then the secretary, starting the collection plate, said the ritual, "There are no dues or fees, but we are self-supporting..." and when the plate came back to him we all rose, joined hands, and said the Lord's Prayer to end the meeting.

Outside, the late June setting sun was glaring through the branches of big evergreens on a ridge to the west of Portland. I started my motorcycle on which I'd ridden up from San Francisco several days before and headed across the city for the campus of Lewis and Clark College where I was teaching for a week. On a street of factories, I was riding between railroad tracks embedded in the pavement when my front wheel was jerked by a switching rail I had not noticed, and my bike went out of control. I hit the rear bumper of a parked car and flew over the handlebars.

A man's voice shouted quite near, "Don't move! Just lay still! Ambulance's already been called."

"OK."

"Good. You're conscious. How do you turn off your motor?"

A woman's face appeared upside down above me as the motor went silent. "Thank God you're alive! What a spill you took!" She disappeared and then reappeared right side up, squeezed between the car I'd hit and a chain link fence my helmet and I had rattled down. She leaned over and put my ignition key in my pocket.

"Thanks."

"They'll be here right quick now," she said. "You stay real quiet."

Flashing lights reflected on her eyeglasses. A thin board was slid under me from my head to my feet, and I was lifted clear of the car and transferred to a stretcher. Sandbags were packed around my head and I was fitted into the back of the ambulance.

I lay in the emergency room, my hipbones and heels going numb and then painful against the hard bed. Another gurney rolled in and stopped near mine, and from the corner of my eye I saw a blond young man, pale and unconscious. The older of two nurses whispered, "This way, do you see?" putting a tube into his nose.

I asked, and she told me, "He took too much of something he shouldn't have taken at all."

The pump started. When it had stopped he woke up and spoke in a childish voice. "That hurts. Stop."

"You're going to be all right," the nurse said.

"No. I don't want to."

"All right now," she said, and he began to sob.

She asked me if I'd like a pillow under my heels and put one there before I'd answered.

A policeman tipped his cap, leaning down to me, then held his calling card before my eyes, then a garage receipt for my bike. He tucked the papers into the pocket of my jacket at the foot of the bed. "If there's a problem," he said, "you have my card."

My X-rays showed nothing broken. Skin was torn on my hands and legs and more of me was bruised and sprained, but I could leave the hospital. I walked slowly to the reception room to wait for a taxi. Pain pills floated my eyesight and hearing.

A young Indian was sitting in a wheelchair, and next to him, a fat, white teenager. All four of their hands were identically wrapped in gauze, but his bandages were soaked red. She asked, "You know what time it is? What happened to you?"

She said, "This is the worst hospital I ever saw. Jeez, so slow."

Someone signaled her and she wheeled the Indian out of the room, pushing his chair with her forearms. She came back alone. "Bunch of jerks in this place. You think they give a shit?"

"Yes."

"Shit, they do. Just leave him sit there." She wiped her eyes on her wrists.

The taxi driver edged around or over the bumps, accelerated and braked very gently, but still I groaned. When we had stopped in the dormitory's parking lot he came around to my side. "How much is that?"

"Doesn't cost you a cent. Police Department, City of Portland, has a fund for it."

"No." I reached for a tip.

"Forget it, I wouldn't take it. Got your key?"

"Thank you. Thank you, Portland."

With the dawn and another dose of pain pills I slept for several hours. Waking, I knew I could not go on teaching. I shaved somehow, stood under a shower and got some of my clothes on before I went for help.

The students had been told that I had had an accident and their faces, when I came into the room to say good-bye, showed fright and inquisitiveness and, a few of them, blank composure. Later I was sent a poem written immediately after I had left the room by Raymond D. Tumbleson:

No one was listened for, in the bright,
Haloed greeting of his death, still living;
I wanted to say; I wanted to be;
He spoke and wept with nothing said—
No one talked, he was the one who walked,
Who knew, when bled upon the motor.
The wheel, his hand, was blood on his hand—
The finger, the wounded, the blessing I strove
For—you, the dead, the still living.

Tumbleson's face had been one of the blank ones.

I flew to Reno and was driven up into the mountains to my home at Squaw Valley. My wife and children made too much fuss, I felt.

At the end of a week I went to see an orthopedist. He told me that a disc at the base of my neck had been knocked out of place, and he put me into a hospital to be stretched in traction.

I shared the hospital room with Chet, whose right arm and right leg were hoisted in traction, badly broken. Since his torso was naked I could see a swastika tattooed on his chest and an oriental dragon on his good arm.

He had been a passenger in a car driven by a barroom acquaintance some weeks ago. The driver had been killed, but Chet did not mourn him, he cursed him as the cause of his injuries. "Stupid son of a bitch."

Several young women came to visit Chet. None were "his." "Dale told me stop by and see you, Chet." Nice-looking girls but all with unstraightened teeth or cheap clothes or anemia—some sign of poverty. Their news was of scraping through. "I hear Jack got a job in the Safeway warehouse."

"That guy!" said Chet. "He won't last there."

Cars broke down and their owners were too broke to fix them. People were laid off. "He's going down to Vegas to see his uncle. Maybe his uncle will help him."

Of their own lives the feeling was of boredom. "Not much to tell you," but they never said anything very personal. Occasionally Chet would burst out in a negative way. "You can tell that son of a bitch go shove it! He hasn't come to see me in a whole month!"

When they got up to leave he was resentful.

"Dale told me pick him up some car stuff at Sears."

"Sears, huh?" suggestively suspicious. "Well, OK. Tell Dale come by and see me."

A night nurse, small and crisp, took an interest in Chet and asked him respectful questions.

He had dropped out of high school, had joined the Army and had been dishonorably discharged. There had been a prison episode, possibly only the army stockade. Recently he had worked as a security guard.

What did he like to do for recreation? Target practice.

What would he do when he got well? Look for a job.

"Can't you get your old job back?"

He had been celebrating his being fired the evening of his accident. A better job? The Army had started to train him as an electrician, but he hadn't got far with it.

Every night thereafter she had a new thought or bit of information for him. Her husband was a union mason. Perhaps he could speak to someone in the electricians' union.

"Yeah."

There was an electricians' school here in Reno, she discovered. Could he get G.I. Bill help?

"You kidding? With a DD?"

"Still—"

"Forget it!"

She looked at him, silenced, but then said, "I'll find something, Chet. Yes, I will."

The next morning I was told I could go home wearing a neck-bracing collar. "So long," I said to Chet. "Good luck."

He glanced from the TV screen. "So long."

Soon the woman who had put my ignition key in my pocket became a personage in history, as did the thoughtful policeman, the taxi driver, and the emergency room nurse. But what would become of the fat blond teenager with her Indian? The attempted suicide? Where would that swastika lead Chet? And Raymond D. Tumbleson...?

In September I flew up to Portland. At first the BMW felt too heavy and powerful, too eccentric and untrustworthy to enjoy. I started in the afternoon from the repair shop and spent the night at Grant's Pass in southern Oregon, rose early and rode through the chill morning mist lying between the forested hills.

By midmorning all mist and clouds had vanished and I crossed the Siskiyou Summit under a brilliant sky. A little further on, at a turning of the highway, Mount Shasta appeared, rising colossally from the oat-colored ranches on the surrounding plain. Snow shone on its eastern slope. I pulled over, cut the motor, and raised the bike on its stand. The heat of the day surrounded me and I took off my helmet and jacket and lit a cigarette.

The gigantic mountain brought me into focus standing there with the same red helmet and stained leathers that I'd ridden through Prague and Budapest, through Alexander's gates to Istanbul, and through the tunneled mountains of Montenegro. I tugged at the kerchief around my neck to loosen it and felt my skin and sweat and the blood pumping. I laughed at my egocentricity, so small a thing in this scale. Yet I felt so good.

I could smell the ranch cattle and see the dust rising behind a haymow, and over Shasta's peak came a puff of cumulus like a halo. I loved my wife and children. Loved them! And friends. One came to mind sweltering in his house behind a sand dune on Long Island, probably wondering where he'd left his shoes. And another trimming his avocado tree in his backyard in Hayward. Sam, who worked for me in Accra twenty some years ago. "If Dakar were not a far place to my home I should follow you." So many spirit wires of affection! And I could, if I chose, ride this highway to Tierra del Fuego. Thousands of the earth's rich miles.

Did I sufficiently love that alcoholic Indian who hated my whiteness? Yes! How about Chet? Much harder. I laughed again, feeling rueful, feeling an airy lightness over my rue, feeling infinitesimal but as wide as creation—a great drinker of sunlight!—and got into my jacket, my helmet and gloves, to go on.

Blair Fuller is a New Yorker by birth who, after an early career in marketing with Texaco, spent mostly in West Africa, became a novelist with the publication of *A Far Place*, and an editor of the *Paris Review*. Fuller came to California as a Lecturer in Creative Writing at Stanford University in 1961 and later taught at California State University, Hayward, and as a Fullbright Professor of American Literature at the University of Oran, Algeria. In 1970 he co-founded the Squaw Valley Community of Writers, an annual writers conference, and, as Chair of its non-profit sponsor, developed the Squaw Valley Arts Center. A father of three, he now lives on San Francisco's Potrero Hill.